TANKS

Modern Military Techniques

Aircraft Carriers
Amphibious Techniques
Fighters
Tanks

MODERN MILITARY TECHNIQUES

TANKS

Ian V. Hogg

Illustrations by
Peter Sarson & Tony Bryan

Lerner Publications Company • Minneapolis

Library of Congress Cataloging in Publication Data

Hogg, Ian V., 1926-
Tanks.

(Modern military techniques)
Includes index.
Summary: A survey of the evolution of modern armored
tanks, now equipped with computerized electronics, night
vision air filtration, and laser fire control systems,
and their tasks and tactics today.
1. Tanks (Military science)—Juvenile literature.
[1. Tanks (Military science)] I. Sarson, Peter, ill.
II. Bryan, Tony, ill. III. Title. IV. Series.
UG446.5.H593 1985 358'.18 84-9650
ISBN 0-8225-1378-1 (lib. bdg.)

Manufactured in the United States of America

1 2 3 4 5 6 7 8 9 10 93 92 91 90 89 88 87 86 85

CONTENTS

1 The First Tanks

In late 1914, Britain and France were fighting Germany on a line which ran from Switzerland to the North Sea, a line made from trenches dug deep into the earth and protected from attack by machine guns and massive thickets of barbed wire. The advancing infantry was stopped by the barbed wire, and then the machine guns opened fire and wiped out the trapped men before they could move to safety. It seemed to be a stalemate.

A British officer, Lt.-Col. Ernest Swinton, thought about this problem and concluded that what was needed was "a power-driven, bullet-proof armed engine capable of destroying machine guns, of crossing country and trenches, of breaking through wire entanglements, and of climbing earthworks." As he came to this conclusion, he recalled seeing some Holt tractors pulling heavy guns. The Holt tractor, built in the USA from a British idea, used an endless steel track passing around its small wheels to give it grip and allow it to cross over rough country. If the Holt tractor could be armorplated for protection, and if it could carry a machine gun, this might be the engine he needed to cross wire and trenches.

The first tank ran under its own power for the first time on January 12, 1916. Driven by a gasoline engine, it had tracks running all round the body and was steered by two wheels that were pulled behind it and operated by steel ropes. On each side was a "sponson," an armored bay that mounted a six-pounder gun or a machine gun. It could move at a walking pace, climb embankments, cross trenches, and crush wire underneath its tracks.

At much the same time, the French had developed two designs of their own. The Schneider tank carried a 75mm gun on one side, while the St.

Below: One of the first British tanks in action in Flanders. The wheels at the rear were for steering, and the "cage" on top of the tank was to prevent grenades being thrown on to the roof. The Mark I tank had a crew of eight men, two six-pounder guns, and four machine guns.

Chamond tank (bottom right) carried one in its nose. Neither proved very successful, and the French then turned to a Renault design that carried only two men, a driver and a gunner, and was armed with a single machine gun.

The first tanks went into action at the Battle of the Somme on September 15, 1916. Due to mechanical breakdowns, only 20 tanks managed to get into the fight. But their appearance caused panic in the German lines, and individual tanks managed to make some impressive penetrations of the wire and trenches. Heavy artillery fire eventually stopped them, though not before they had shown that they held considerable promise of revolutionizing warfare.

The principal problem was the condition of the battlefield. Heavy artillery fire had torn up the ground, and rain had turned it into a sea of mud in which the tanks could scarcely move. But in November 1917, the Tank Corps was given the chance to fight on firm and unbroken ground at Cambrai and made an impressive breakthrough. Unfortunately, there were not enough troops to take advantage of the break, and, after a week of struggling, a German counter-attack drove back the exhausted British.

The first tanks had shown that the idea was sound and that an armored gun-carrier could override wire and trenches and deliver the infantry to their objective. There were still many problems to be overcome, however, some of which were to take years to solve. But the tank had arrived on the battlefield and intended to stay there.

Construction of the first machine was done by a company called Fosters, who had made agricultural machinery for several years. The designers referred to it variously as a "Landship" or a "Trench Crossing Machine." But because of the secrecy surrounding the idea, the workmen were told that the machine was to be a water-carrier for use in the desert. As a result, they began referring to it as "that tank thing," and, when a name had to be found for the finished machine, it was called a "tank" in order to conceal its real purpose.

The French Schneider tank had a crew of six men and was armed with a 75mm gun and a single Hotchkiss machine gun on each side of the hull. Driven by a 55 hp gasoline engine, it had a speed of about 4 mph (6.5 km) on a hard surface. Just over 400 were built between 1916 and 1918, and they were first used in action at the Chemin des Dames in April 1917. Very vulnerable to fire (the gasoline tanks were alongside the machine gun positions), many were disarmed and converted into supply tanks.

The French St. Chamond tank had a crew of eight men and was armed with a 75mm gun and four Hotchkiss machine guns, one at the front, one on each side, and one at the rear. Each track was powered by a separate electric motor, the power coming from a dynamo driven by a gasoline engine so that each track could be operated independently for steering. It was first used in May 1917, but the short length of track meant that most of them got stuck when trying to cross trenches. About 400 were built and many were modified in order to try and improve their cross-country performance.

2
The Early Tank Battles

Below: The first tank tactic, designed to break into the German lines. The first pair of tanks (top) with infantry behind them, break through the wire and then turn to drive down the trench, firing at the occupants while the infantry "mop up." The next pair of tanks move through the gaps and go to the second line (bottom) where one takes up a protective position while the other turns and begins to drive down the trench.

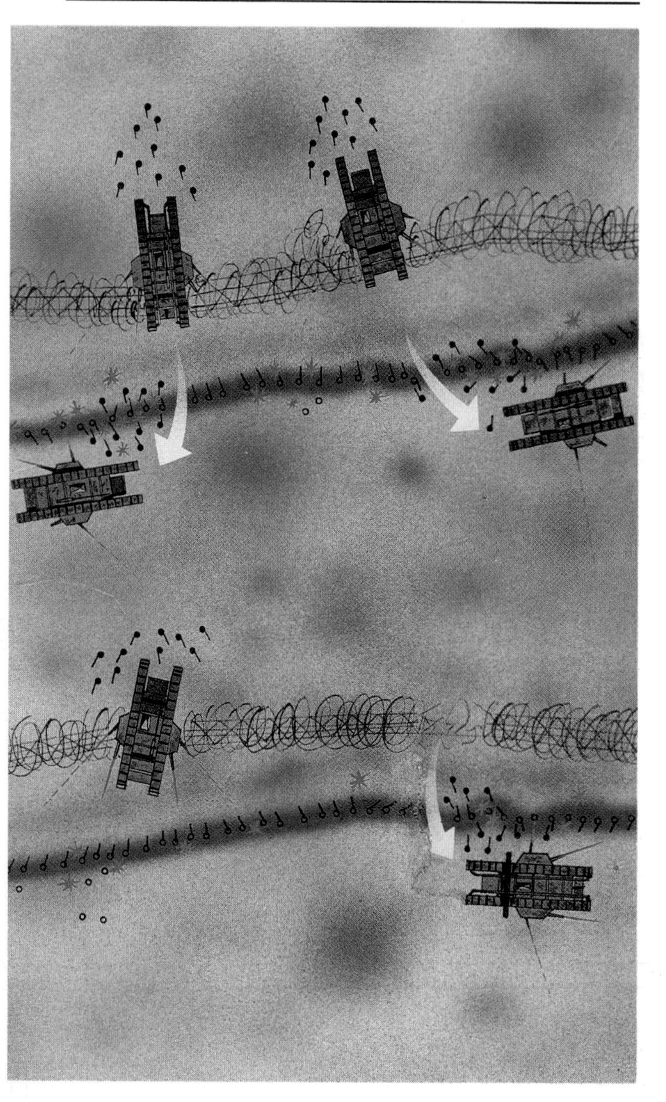

Before the tank actually went into action, Colonel Swinton had worked out ways of using it. In its early days, the tank was not very reliable, and so it was decided that it must never work alone but in twos or fours for mutual support. Taking a pair as being the basic unit, their task was to break through the trench line and then widen the gap so that the infantry could follow them through. To do this, their basic maneuver was to crush down the barbed wire, cross the trench, and then swing to one side and drive down the length of the trench, shooting at the men in it and driving them away from the gap. The trenches were not simple ditches. They had covered "dugouts" and shelters in which the defenders could hide from the tank's gunfire, reappearing when the tank had passed. To stop this, the tank had to be closely followed by a "mopping-up" squad, throwing bombs into the dugouts before the occupants came out again. Since this squad had to keep close to the tank, it had to be followed by another larger squad that occupied and defended the trench as it was won.

With this simple operation as the basis, there were various refinements that could be added. With four tanks, two could move to the right and two to the left, making an even larger gap. Or two could move right and left while the other two went ahead to deal with the next trench. Or two could move right and left while two stayed in the gap to protect the infantry coming through. There were many possibilities.

The Battle of Messines in June 1917 was probably the first time that tanks were used in accordance with Swinton's rules, and they performed the drills immaculately, crushing the wire, swinging right and left to clear trenches, moving ahead in unison with the infantry following. By the end of the first day's advance, the entire German trench line was in Allied hands. The German counter-attack on the following day was driven off, and the Messines ridge stayed in Allied hands until the spring of 1918.

For the Battle of Cambrai, new ideas were put into action. Tanks carried large bundles of brushwood called "fascines," which they dropped into wide trenches to form bridges that they could cross (top right). Other tanks were fitted with long wire ropes and hooks that they dropped into the barbed wire (bottom right). Then they reversed, uprooting the wire and pulling it clear. Others had their guns removed and were used to bring ammunition, food, and water to the forward troops. The artillery, instead of bombarding the entire area for days beforehand, did not fire until the tanks moved forward and then confined their bombardment to the German gun batteries in the area that might interfere with the advance. Using smoke and gas shells, they forced the German gunners away from their guns and prevented them from seeing what was going on. In front of the advancing tanks, they fired a rolling barrage of shrapnel, which kept German machine gunners and observers under cover as the tanks closed with them.

The standard British tank moved at only four miles per hour, but several people saw the need for a fast tank to replace cavalry for scouting. One of the designers of the first tank, Sir William Tritton, devised his "Tritton Chaser," the first tank to have a turret raised above the body, though this turret did not revolve. The other remarkable thing was that it had two engines, one to drive each track, and was steered by slowing down or speeding up one or the other engine. Fitted with four machine guns, it went into service late in 1917 as the "Whippet" and was the first light tank.

Right: A tank carrying a "fascine," a bundle of wooden stakes tightly bound with wire and held so that it could be released from inside the tank. On arriving at a trench too wide for the tank to span, the fascine was released to fall into the trench so as to fill the gap and give support to the tank as it crossed. If the trench were very large, the tank would withdraw and another would drive up to drop another fascine. This would be repeated until the gap was filled sufficiently to permit the tanks to cross.

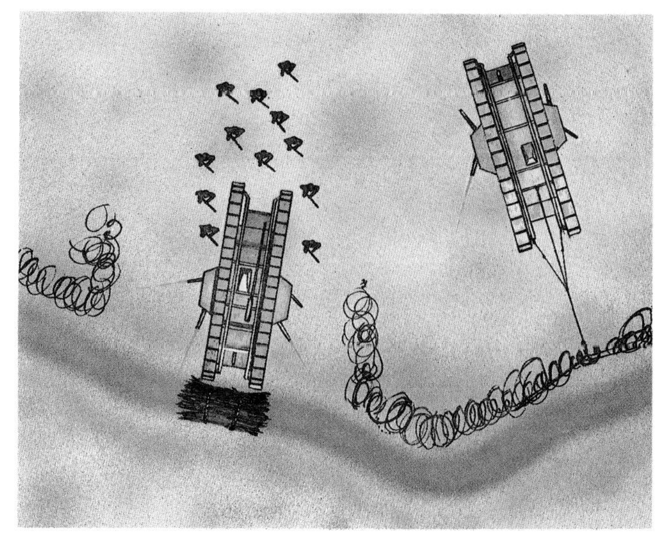

Right: A diagram showing two tanks dealing with obstacles. One has dropped its fascine into the trench and is about to cross, followed by a party of infantry soldiers. The other has attached a grapnel to the barbed wire entanglement and is about to pull and uproot the wire so as to make a gap for more infantry to pass through.

3 The Weapon of the Future

At the end of the war, there were several different ideas about what a tank should be and what it should do. The British favored a heavy tank, well-armed and armored, which moved slowly and went ahead of the infantry to protect them. The French were in favor of a very light and fast tank, armed only with a machine gun, which they could build by the hundred and use in swarms, screening the infantry, dashing ahead to spy out the land, and acting simply as mobile machine gunners. But each idea had washed over to the other side, so that the French had built a few heavy tanks and the British were trying out light tanks when the war ended. The first important design to appear was the British "Medium D,'' which lowered the hull so that the turret carrying the machine guns was above the line of the body.

The heavy tank idea was advanced by the development of the "Vickers Independent" tank (below). During the war, British tanks had been built to military designs, but the Vickers company, long renowned for developing guns and armaments of all kinds, began designing tanks of their own. It was called the "Independent" because it was intended to be so powerful that it could operate by itself without infantry. Weighing over 30 tons, it had no less than five revolving turrets.

At the front were two machine-gun turrets; in the middle, the main turret with a 3-pounder gun; and at the back were two more machine gun turrets. It required an eight-man crew to operate it and demanded very complex communications between the commander and his men so that they could work together. It proved too expensive for

Below: The Vickers Independent tank had an 8-man crew and five gun turrets. The British did not use it, but several other armies copied it.

Above: This Morris-Martel Tankette was built privately in 1925, using automobile parts and a wooden body. The idea had to be abandoned when it was realized that one man could not drive the tank and fire the gun at the same time.

Above: The American Christie tank relied mainly on speed. Powered by a 350 hp airplane engine, it could reach 67 mph (112 km/h) but was unreliable. It could operate with or without its tracks.

the British Army and none were bought, but several other nations copied the idea in the 1920s.

The other extreme was the French idea of swarms of small tanks, and a British officer, Maj. G. le Q. Martel, designed and built a one-man tank in his garage from pieces of trucks and automobiles (above left). The one-man crew drove the tank and was provided with a heavy machine gun. Four were built for testing, but it was soon proved that one man could not do two jobs, so the one-man tank was soon abandoned. However, two-man tanks were made in some numbers.

In the USA, a man called Walter Christie was attracted to the idea of using speed as a means of protection — if the tank was fast, it would be harder to hit. He developed a number of light tanks powered by aircraft engines, and he perfected a way of using large wheels to support the track. These wheels could move vertically to overcome obstacles, and the track could be removed to allow the tank to be driven on its wheels on roads, thus preventing the tracks from wearing out quickly (above right). Some of Christie's ideas were ambitious, such as his "flying tank" that could be carried under an airplane. It was fitted with wings and a tail and could be dropped from a low altitude to glide down and then drop off its wings to go into action. If confronted with an obstacle, it could fit its wings, gather speed, and fly over the obstacle. Needless to say, these ideas never got into practical form.

Not everybody was in favor of tanks, especially the cavalrymen who could see that, sooner or later, their job would be done by armored vehicles. But they did not give up without a struggle, as this verse from a poem in a military magazine of 1931 shows:

> The dear old horse is going,
> you can see it in his eye.
> As long as we have horses though,
> the Country will not die.
> Off to your stinking petrol fumes;
> go to your grease and oil!
> When engines cease to function,
> then the horse will start to toil.

4 Preparing for War

As war came closer in 1939, tanks owned by the principal armies of the world tended to reflect the various ideas held about how tanks should be used.

The British army believed that there were two roles for the tank: first, supporting the infantry as they had done in the First World War and, second, acting independently as a fast striking force to carry out raids. As a result, they had two types of tank, the "Infantry" and "Cruiser." The infantry tank in service was the Valentine (top left), heavily armored and slow to accompany marching troops. The "Cruiser" was faster and less well protected, relying on speed to keep out of trouble. There were also numbers of Vickers Medium and Light tanks. The former was an attempt to develop a tank capable of acting in both roles, while the latter was a small fast tank designed to act as a cavalry scout.

The French had decided that the tank was solely to support infantry and, therefore, all their designs, except for a few two-man Renaults left over from 1918, were heavy, well-armored, and slow. The "Char B" (bottom left) was the most powerful tank in the world at that time, while the Renault and Somua designs were probably the most technically advanced.

The German army had given a great deal of thought to tanks between the wars and, having had only a handful when the war ended and having had them all scrapped, were able to begin with a clean sheet of paper and design to their own tactical ideas. Their theory of the use of tanks was based on making a completely self-contained armored formation of tanks, artillery, and infantry that could operate on its own. Their aim was speed, by which they could surprise an enemy and defeat him before he could react, and firepower, by which they could beat down any opposition. They had two principal tanks, the "Panzer 1," which was light and armed with a fast-firing 20mm cannon, and the "Panzer 3" (top right), which was heavier but armed with a powerful 50mm gun.

Although nobody knew it at the time, the Russians had more tanks than the rest of the world, and they had such a large army that they were able to try out various ideas. They had heavy tanks with multiple turrets, heavy tanks with single turrets, light fast tanks using the suspension designed by Christie, and even amphibious tanks that could swim rivers (bottom right). They were also on the point of designing a completely new tank, called the T-34, which would be fast, well-protected, and well-armed. This was such a good design that it was to become the model for most of the world in later years. But this was still unknown in 1939.

The German, Russian, and Italian tank designers managed to get some practical experience before 1939 by sending numbers of their tanks to fight in the Spanish Civil War. All learned lessons, but some learned the wrong ones. The Germans realized that anti-tank guns were the main threat, which led them to develop excellent guns for use after 1939. The Italians learned that tanks and infantry had to be closely controlled so that the tanks did not outrun the foot soldiers and leave them unprotected. The Russians decided that massed tanks were useless and, as a result, disbanded their tank divisions in Russia and parceled the tanks out to infantry companies, which proved an expensive mistake when the Germans invaded Russia in 1941.

1 The German Panzer 3, designed by Daimler-Benz, was built from 1936 to 1943.

2 The British "Valentine" tank served from 1938 to 1944.

3 The French "Char B1" had a 75mm gun in the hull and a 47mm gun in the turret.

4 The Soviet T-37 amphibious tank was a useful reconnaissance vehicle.

1 Panzer 3

2 Valentine

3 Char B1

4 T-37

5 Blitzkrieg

When the German army attacked Poland in 1939, its spearhead was a collection of six armored divisions with 3195 well-designed and reliable tanks operated by one of the best-trained armies in history. Against them the Poles had 1065 tanks of doubtful efficiency, the best of which had not been in service long enough for their operators to get used to them. The result was a massive victory for Germany and a shock for the rest of the world.

The shock was due to the fact that the rest of the world was still thinking of war in terms of trenches, mud, and slow infantry advances. But the German high-speed advance, or "Blitzkrieg" (Lightning War), was something totally new. The German armored units simply drove ahead, shouldering resistance aside. Whenever they were stopped, they called up dive-bombers and artillery to pound the obstacle while the tanks simply flowed around it and carried on with their advance, leaving the obstacle to be dealt with by the supporting infantry. Their campaign was not planned, as campaigns had been in previous wars, as a series of broad advances of the "front line," gradually sweeping forward and absorbing the enemy territory. Instead each armored group was given an objective and a route and left to get ahead. So the map of the campaign, instead of showing a solid line of advance, became a series of swooping arrowheads as each column swept towards its target. Several columns were given the same objective but different routes so that as they circled around, they scooped up and surrounded the Polish troops and captured them.

The German Blitzkrieg thus became a series of swift carving strikes that cut up the opposition into small pieces, and the soldiers of the rest of the world were confronted with a new way of fighting wars.

Before they could think of a suitable response, the Germans repeated the performance, this time in the west, striking through Belgium and Holland to capture France. Again, a series of armored thrusts dissected the Allied positions, separated them, and defeated them piece by piece.

The Polish campaign had taught the Germans some useful lessons. They found that their light Panzer 1 tanks were of little use, but the Panzer 3, and a newer design, the Panzer 4, were excellent designs. As a result, they gradually dropped the light tanks from service and concentrated on the heavier models, which had the required combination of gun power, protection, and speed.

The Allies learned the same lesson but only by being defeated in France. The trouble was that they had spread their available tanks across the borders of France, a company here and a squadron there, so that when the German columns broke through, there was never sufficient Allied tank strength to stop them. The speed of the German advance meant that before the Allies could collect tanks together and move them to the threatened area, the Germans had captured it and moved on. The heavy infantry tanks were found to be too slow, and the light scouting tanks were too vulnerable. It was time to start redesigning.

At that time, the British designs going into production had been started before the war began. But due to their hasty design, they had several faults. The worst fault was that the gun was a 40 mm 2-pounder because only this was small enough to fit into the turrets. It was already becoming obvious that this was not powerful enough. Another fault was that many of the mechanical parts — the engines and transmissions — had not been sufficiently tested, and the tanks were unreliable in service. Not until a bigger turret and a bigger gun were available and the tanks could be made more reliable could the British hope to meet the Germans on equal terms.

The German panzers did not always have things their own way. Near Arras, a mixed force of British "Matilda" and French "Somua" infantry tanks fell on the tail of a Panzer column and gave it a severe mauling. The German anti-tank guns made little impression, for the Matilda and Somua

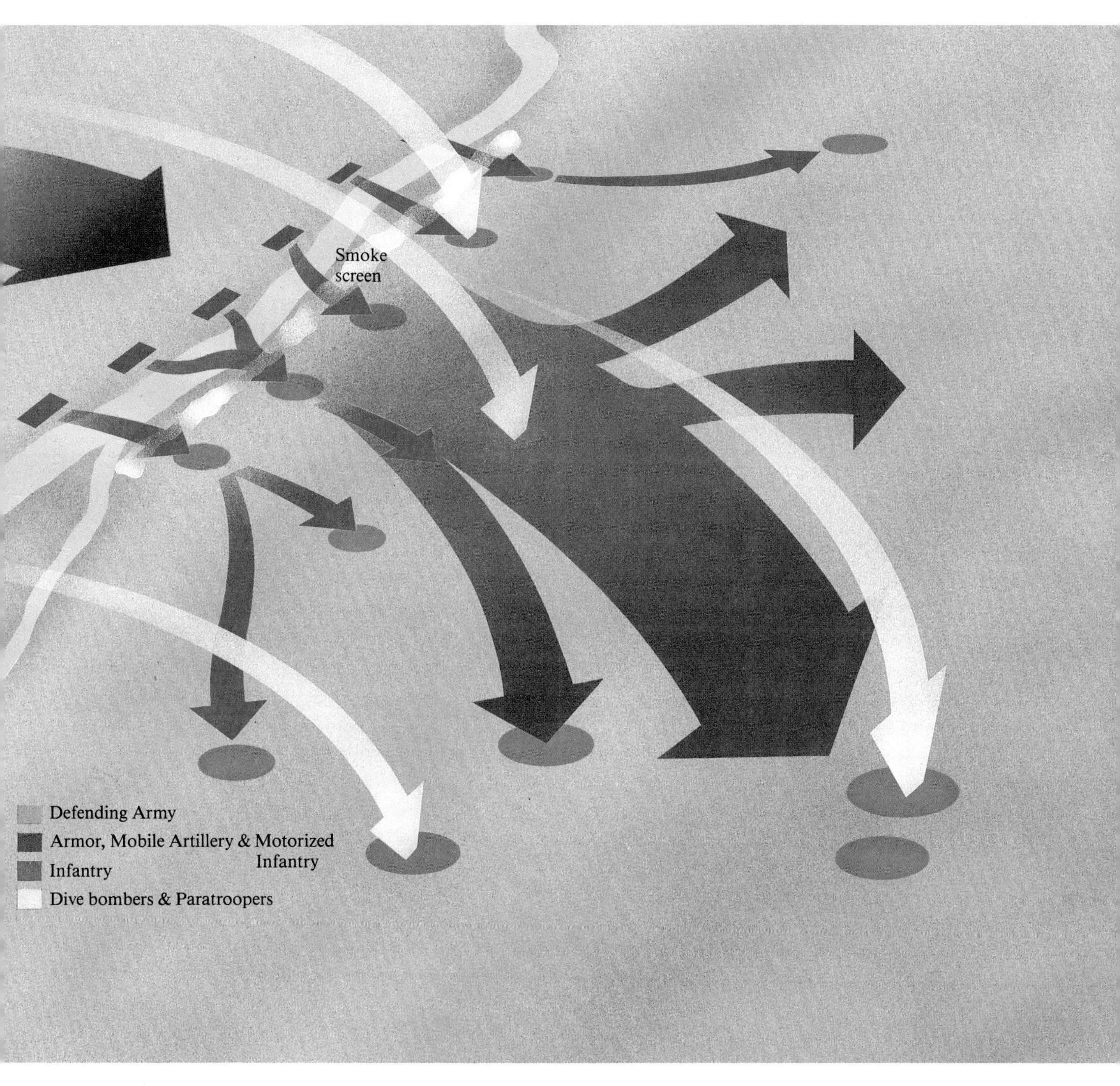

were probably the best-armored tanks of the period. The Germans, in desperation, brought up an 88mm anti-aircraft gun, which proved to be the only weapon capable of stopping the Matilda. They remembered this, and set about redesigning this gun into an anti-tank weapon which was to prove one of the most dangerous guns of the war.

Above: The Blitzkrieg technique: the initial attack (red) crosses the river and makes a bridgehead, then allows the second wave (black) to pass through. The third wave (white) has specific targets, or it can assist the other waves in breaking hard defenses. Instead of a continuous line of advance, each unit has its own objective.

6 Russian Armor

When the Soviet army began to take shape after the Russian Revolution of 1917, it placed tanks high on its list of requirements and planned to have an armored force of 3500 tanks and armored cars by 1934. They had two lines of approach: first, to develop designs entirely their own, and, second, to dissect foreign designs, take the best features, and incorporate these into new designs.

The Vickers Medium was put straight into Soviet service as the "English Workman" tank and the Vickers Six-Ton as the "T-26." The British Carden-Lloyd two-man tank was also copied and some 4000 made. But the most important development was based on the American Christie tank with its big-wheel suspension that promised fast travel over rough country. The design was copied and became the "BT-2" (BT standing for "fast tank" in Russian) and was gradually improved to the BT-7 model. There was also a heavy multiple-turret tank based on the Vickers "Independent" and large numbers were built. But when war came, they were found impossible to command properly.

By 1939 the Russian designers knew what they wanted: a heavy tank and a fast medium tank. The heavy tank was the KV-1, a 46-ton tank that carried a 76mm gun and could move at 24 mph (40 km/h) (below left). The fast medium tank was the T-34 (below right), the ultimate development of the

Below: The Soviet KV-1 heavy tank was an advanced design using torsion bar suspension and armed with a powerful 76mm gun. With armor up to 4 inches (100mm) thick and a 600 hp diesel engine, it weighed 46 tons and could travel at 24 mph (40 km/h). It was a sound design which had room for improvement; in later years it had armor up to 5 inches (130mm) thick and an 85mm gun.

Christie idea, which carried the same 76mm gun, weighed 26 tons, and traveled at 30 mph (50 km/h). The designers had taken care over details. The engines were air-cooled diesels that would not freeze up in Russian winters and would run on any sort of fuel. The bodies had sloped surfaces so that shot and shell were more likely to bounce off rather than penetrate the armor. The long-barrelled gun was extremely powerful and accurate. The inside of the tank was kept simple so that they could be made quickly and operated easily.

In June 1941 the German army set out across the Russian border. In the first days, they rolled the Soviet army back, capturing thousands of prisoners. The tanks the Germans met were mainly the old T-26 and BT-7 types, and they were easily dealt with. But when the KV-1 and T-34 came into use, they gave the Germans a terrible shock. These tanks were almost impossible to stop. Their guns were so powerful, they could knock out German tanks before the Germans were close enough to use their own guns, and the Soviet armor was so thick and well-shaped that German shot bounced off. Only heavy artillery in ambush positions could guarantee stopping these new Soviet tanks.

The first German encounter with the T-34 tank was frightening. The 17th Panzer Division reported that "a strange low-slung tank of formidable appearance" appeared out of the brushwood near the Dniepr River. With German shot and shell bouncing off its sloped armor, it roared forward, crushing a 37mm anti-tank gun beneath its tracks, blowing up two Panzer 2s, and tearing through the front line. It left a nine-mile trail of destruction behind before it was finally stopped by being blasted at short range by a heavy howitzer.

Below: The Soviet T-34 was probably the best tank of the war years, having an almost ideal combination of gun (76mm), armor (50mm), and power (500 hp) for a weight of 26 tons. It had many components of the KV-1 to simplify manufacture and, like the KV-1 was improved as time went on. By the end of the war, it had 3 inches (75mm) of armor and an 85mm gun. Many are still in use today.

7
Tank Tactics

The new "Blitzkrieg" meant that new methods of using tanks had to be developed. But when war came in 1939, few solutions had been found and most tank tactics still reflected the attitudes of the army which practiced them. The British, for example, had converted many cavalry regiments into tank regiments, and the cavalry traditions of dash and bravado were carried over into the armored force. In the deserts of North Africa in 1941-42, these tactics were put into effect with mixed results. Against the Italian army, which was poorly equipped, and, for the most part, not very interested in the war anyway, dash and bravado worked very well, effectively breaking up the Italian columns. The desert gave ample space for wide and sweeping maneuvers, so that squadrons of tanks could be handled almost like fleets of ships at sea. And by a series of bold out-flanking sweeps, the British were able to place tanks into ambush positions and use light tanks like a cavalry screen to harry Italian columns. Against the German army, however, they failed completely. The supporters of the "dash" school expected the enemy to either give up or come out to meet the attack, in which case the battle would then become a sort of one-to-one fight between pairs of tanks. But the Germans, wisely, saw no profit in that. Once they understood the British tactics, they simply dug anti-tank guns and artillery into the ground as a screen in front of their defensive positions and waited for the British to appear. As soon as they did so, a handful of German tanks would drive around inside their own area, tempting the British armor into making a charge at them. Once the British were well on their way, the German guns would open up from their concealed positions and rip the British attack to pieces without any German tanks becoming involved.

One defensive tactic which had great effect on tank tactics was the use of minefields. The open spaces of the desert gave room for millions of mines to be buried in huge fields, which prevented tanks from operating over large areas. This meant that either the minefield had to be cleared of mines before an attack or that the attack had to move in areas where there were no mines. These mine-free areas were, of course, watched over by anti-tank guns and tanks so that the minefield forced the enemy to adapt his tactics to the defender's rules. The German use of minefields was a large factor in forcing the British to re-think their "cavalry" tactics.

The root of the trouble lay in the guns with which the two sides were equipped. British designers had assumed that the tank's task was to attack other tanks, and they had given the British tanks a 40mm gun with an armor-piercing shot. The Germans, on the other hand, decided that their tanks needed to be able to support infantry and gave them a 75mm gun which fired an armor-piercing shot and also a powerful high explosive shell. Moreover, being a bigger gun, it had a longer range. So when British and German tanks met, the Germans could stop and begin shelling the British at a range the British could not match with their smaller guns. And if the British tried to lay an ambush with anti-tank guns (which were the same 40mm weapons), the German tanks could stay out of their range and bombard them with explosives. Success only came when the British were able to mount heavier guns on the tanks and provide infantry with heavier anti-tank guns.

The German invasion of Russia in 1941 began at breakneck speed as four Panzer groups set about splitting up and surrounding the Soviet armies just as they had done in Poland and France. At first, the surprise and force of the tank groups simply rolled over the Soviet defenses or swept them aside to be "mopped up" by the following infantry. The Soviet tank forces were split up in small groups under command of infantry regiments and could not assemble a decisive force to stand against the Panzer advance.

The Russians have always believed in defeating any enemy by two things peculiar to their situation — space and men — both in plentiful supply in Russia. As the Germans advanced, the Russians fell back, destroying every house, barn, tree, or field as they went, leaving the Germans an immense space full of nothing. This meant that everything they needed — food, fuel, supplies of every sort — had to be brought from Germany across thousands of miles of wasteland. This demanded men, vehicles, and fuel, all of which had to be taken from the supplies that should have gone to the front line. Eventually the Russians would decide to make a stand, and here they would dig in hundreds of artillery guns in a pattern of defense: the light anti-tank guns at the front, medium field guns next, then heavy artillery at the rear. These would go into action as the German advance came close. The long-range guns would open up first, thinning out the attack; then the field guns; and, finally, the short range anti-tank guns would deal with those tanks which had managed to get as far as the line of resistance. When the Russians decided the Germans had been stretched to breaking point, they would throw in tens of thousands of troops, thousands of guns, and hundreds of tanks in a concentrated mass that swamped the Germans, and cut them off from their supply lines.

The eventual defeat of the German army was due, as much as anything else, to the triumph of quantity over quality. The German Panzers lost not because they had bad tanks or because they had lost their skill, but simply because the Allies could build tanks faster than the Germans could. The first German advances into Russia had over-run many tank factories, and many more were at risk. So over the winter of 1941, the factories lying west of the Ural Mountains were entirely dismantled and moved by train to new locations east of the mountains, where it was hoped they would be safe from the German invasion. Here factories were combined into huge tank-producing combines. In Britain and the USA, automobile and railway locomotive factories were taken over and converted to tank production, and completely new factories were built. From 1939 to 1945, the German industry built 23,487 tanks. In the same period, the British built 27,000; the Americans, 88,276; and the Russians, a staggering 109,700.

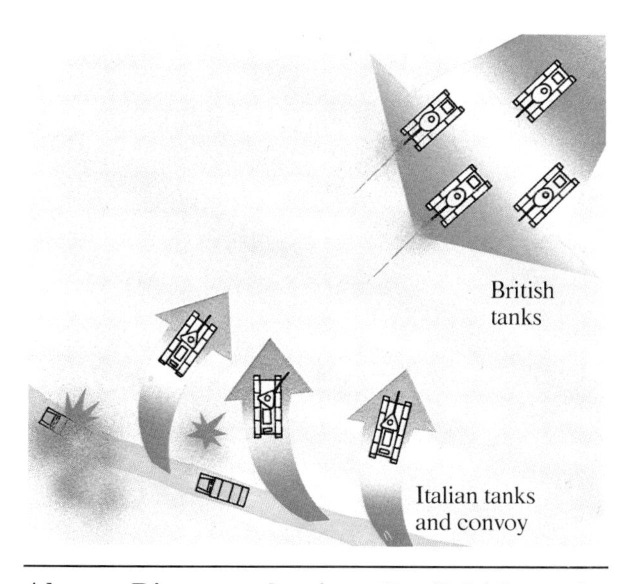

Above: Diagram showing the British tanks making a dash against the Italian army in North Africa in 1941-42

British tanks charging Germans

German tanks driving around inside their area

German anti-tank guns

Above: Diagram showing how the Germans set up the British in the 1941-42 war in North Africa, by enticing them to make a charge towards the Germans' concealed anti-tank guns

8 The Funnies

When the Allies made plans to invade Europe, they knew they would have to land on defended beaches. But there was no other way to get heavy weapons into Europe. In 1942 a raid against Dieppe had been supported by a number of heavy "Churchill" tanks. But after landing on the beach, they found they were stopped by various obstacles, which they could neither climb over nor blast away. So they stayed on the beach, giving very little of their planned support. This lesson was not lost on the invasion planners.

The problems facing a landing force were first, getting the tanks on to the beach and then getting them inland past ditches, walls, and minefields.

These problems were all to be solved by specialized types of tank, which were known in the British army as "The Funnies."

To get ashore, swimming tanks were evolved. Amphibious tanks were not new, but these were all intended for crossing rivers, not plowing through choppy seas. Moreover, all existing amphibious tanks were light, thinly armored, and without heavy guns, so they would be useless once they were ashore. The "Duplex Drive" or "DD" tank (above left) was a standard type of tank, usually Sherman with 75mm gun, with a heavy canvas screen attached to the edge of the hull and stretched out vertically until it was higher than the roof of the turret. The space so enclosed added to the buoyancy of the tank and allowed it to float. A propeller at the rear end was driven from the tank's gearbox (which is why they were called "Duplex Drive") and pushed the tank through the water at about 4 knots. Once it left the water, a small explosive charge ripped the screen away and the tank was ready for action. These tanks could then hold the first landing areas until heavier "tank landing craft," flat-bottomed boats with ramps in the front, could come up to the shore and allow their cargo of tanks to drive on to the beach.

The first off the landing craft would be the next novelty, the "Flail" tank (below right). This carried a revolving drum in front to which lengths of chain were attached. As the tank advanced, the drum revolved and the chains were flung round to thrash the ground ahead of the tank. If there were any mines buried there, the thrashing chains would set them off before the tank reached them. The flail tanks drove up the beach leaving a pathway upon which other vehicles could drive safely.

At the end of the beach, the most likely obstacle would be a ditch. For this, the 1917 "fascine" was revived (center right). If the ditch was too big, two fascines would be dropped in, followed by a tank with a bridge deck on top instead of a turret. This would drive into the ditch, settle on top of the fascines, and the other tanks could then drive over it.

If the obstacle was a vertical wall, it could be dealt with by a "Petard," a tank carrying a special gun that fired a huge explosive bomb against the wall, or by a "Goat," a tank that carried a frame on its front that held a one-ton charge of explosive. The "Goat" drove up to the wall, pressed the frame against the concrete, backed away, and fired the charge electrically. Few walls could withstand that.

To destroy bunkers and pill-boxes with anti-tank weapons guarding the exit from the beach, the "Crocodile" was brought up (top right). This carried a flamethrower which could project a jet of flame.

The landing craft unloaded wheeled vehicles — trucks, armored cars, gun tractors — as well as tracked vehicles, and these could find it difficult to drive across the soft sand of the beach. To help them, one of the "Funnies" was the "Carpet" tank that carried a huge roll of heavy canvas on a roller. As it drove off the landing craft, it dropped the end of its "Carpet" and proceeded to drive on to it, unrolling it as it went and leaving a firm track up which the wheeled vehicles could be driven.

1 "Crocodile," the flame-throwing tank. This was a Churchill tank with 75mm gun and a flame-thrower in the hull front. An armored trailer carried 400 gallons of flame liquid together with pressure tanks of nitrogen to force the liquid from the "gun." A range of about 248-360 feet (75-110 meters) could be achieved.

2 Churchill with "fascine." This was a large bundle of brushwood, wrapped with wire, and carried on the deck of the tank with a quick-release gear. On arriving at a ditch, the gear was tripped and the fascine fell into the ditch. More fascines could be added by other tanks until it became possible to drive across the ditch.

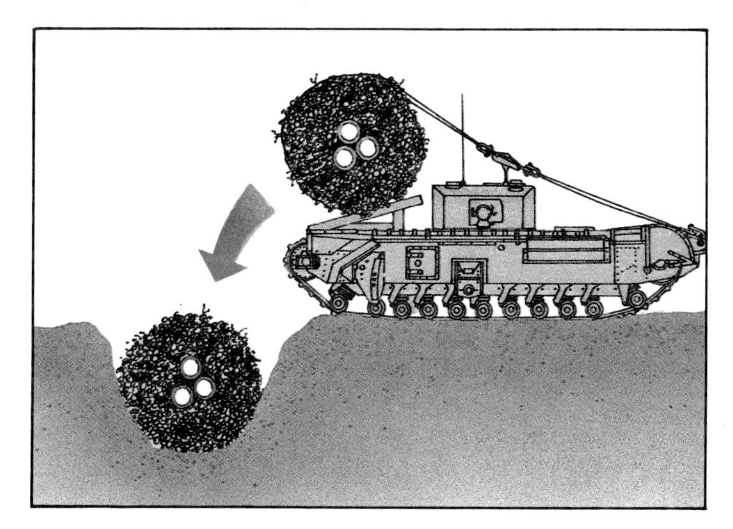

3 Sherman "Crab" mine-clearing tank fitted with a "flail." The cylinder was driven from the tank's transmission, and as it rotated so the chains "flailed" the ground in front, detonating any pressure mines there. The explosion of the mine might damage the chains but was too far in front to damage the tank.

9
The Americans

The principal design feature of the American tanks was their use of radial aircraft engines. This was because conventional engines of sufficient power were too big or too expensive, but it meant that the rear end of the tank, where the engine was located, had to be rather high. The first design to be completed, just as war broke out in Europe in 1939, was the M2 Light Tank (above). This went into production in 1940 and was the tank on which the US Army began training for modern warfare. In 1938 design of the M2 Medium tank was begun. This carried a 37mm gun in its turret, but in June 1940 the US Army decided that a 75mm gun was necessary in any medium tank. The M2 turret could not take such a gun, so a new design was quickly drawn up in which the 75mm gun was fitted into a sponson on the right front of the tank hull. This became the M3 Medium tank and was put into production in April 1941. It was widely used by the British in North Africa in 1942 and was known by them as the "General Lee."

As soon as the M3 design was cleared for production, the Ordnance Department began work on the M4 (right) which was to have a turret carrying the 75mm gun. The first model was hand-built by September 1941 and was ordered into production for early 1942. Called the "General Sherman" by the British, it became the most common Allied tank with 49,234 built in 11 factories. Over 17,000 of these were supplied to the British army and over 4,000 to the Soviet army. After the war, they were bought and used by armies all over the world.

Above: The M2 Light Tank of 1940
Right: The M4 "General Sherman"

In 1938 the US Army had asked for an infantry-supporting heavy tank, and so a 50-tonner with a

3-inch gun in the turret was designed. The first model of this "M6 Heavy" was built late in 1941, but its great weight caused problems with the brakes, and the massive 900 horsepower engine was difficult to cool. By the middle of 1942, these problems had been cured and the M6, weighing 56 tons and with 3 inches (82mm) of armor, was without a doubt the most powerful and best-armed tank there was. But although production of 5,000 was planned, no more than 40 were ever made. The US Army was not enthusiastic about it, one reason being that two M4 Shermans could be shipped abroad in the space needed to ship one M6.

Although the M6 was abandoned, late in 1944 the US Army in Europe demanded a heavy tank once more, and the Ordnance Department was able to produce the M26 "Pershing" quite rapidly. This was officially called a medium tank, but it carried a useful 90mm gun and was well armored with 4½ inches (102mm) of steel on its front.

The National Defense Act of 1921 disbanded the American Tank Corps and decreed that tanks were infantry equipment. This made little difference until the 1930s when the Cavalry began to mechanize and required light tanks. They then discovered that, under the law, they could not have any tanks since tanks were only for infantry. They got around this by calling their light tanks "Combat Cars." In a similar way, when the US Army wanted to organize an armored force in 1940, it found itself up against the same law. This time it got around it by ordering an Armored Force "to be set up for the purposes of service testing." So the US Army went to war in 1941 and fought until 1945, using a "Test Force" as its primary striking force.

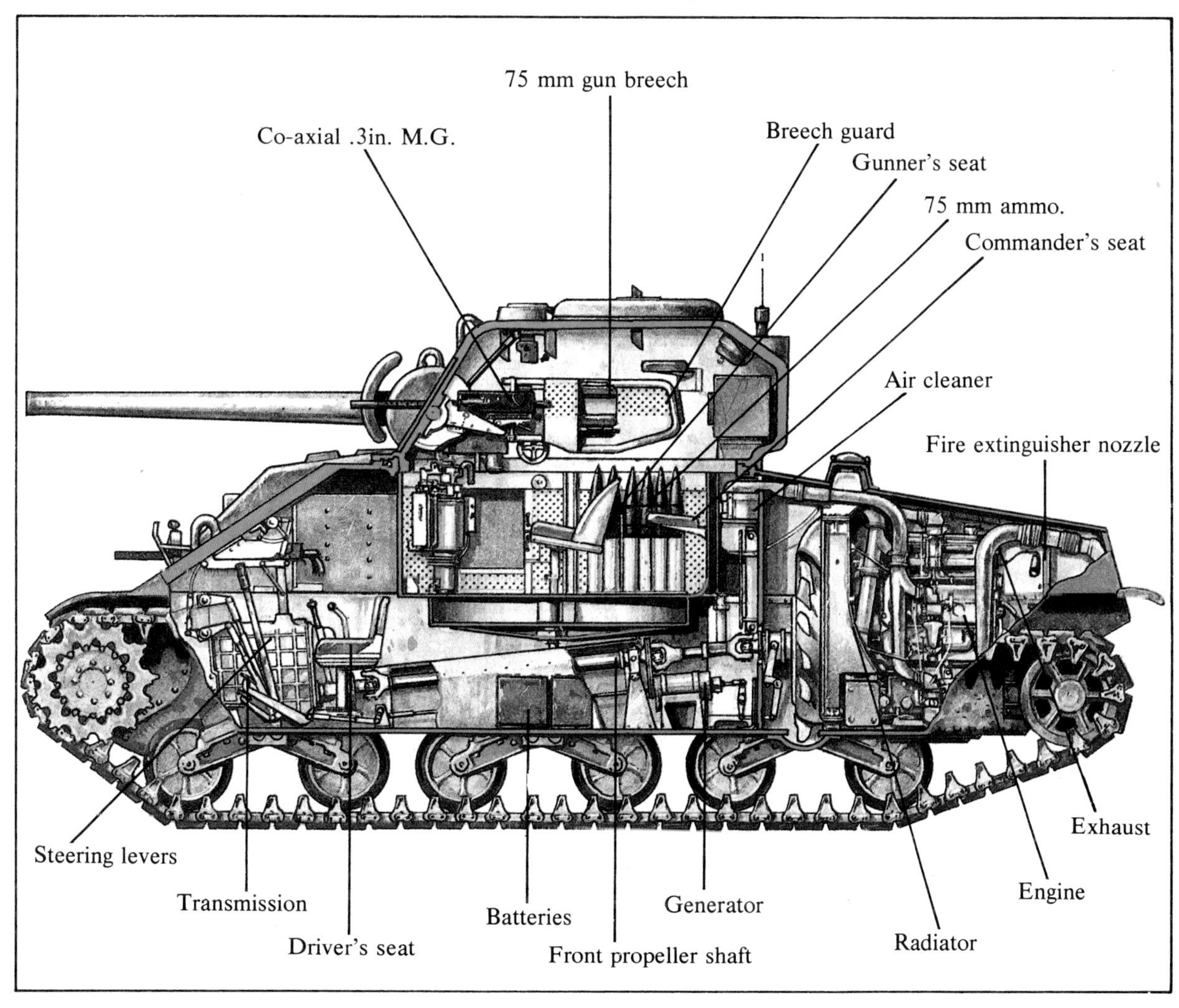

10 Post-War Designs

The American Pershing tank appeared in action just a few days before the war ended. Britain had finally abandoned the artificial distinction between "infantry" and "cruiser" tanks, realizing that it was possible to build an all-round tank capable of combining armor, firepower, and speed. This resulted in the "Centurion" (1), armed with a new 20-pounder (84mm) gun that was just too late to see action in the war. The Russians had also been at work, and at the Victory Parade in Berlin surprised everyone with their new "Josef Stalin" heavy tank (2), an improvement on the KV-1 design with a massive turret and a 122mm gun, the most powerful gun ever mounted in a tank at that time.

All tanks are a mixture of three things: protection, fire-power, and mobility — or armor, gun, and speed — and how these three should be balanced had been the greatest problem facing the designers. In general, the British had aimed at protection first, mobility second, and firepower last, and this had led to some serious failures when British tanks were unable to harm German tanks because of their inferior guns. The Americans tended to put mobility first, then firepower, and then protection, leading to designs which were highly maneuverable and mechanically reliable but barely adequate in gunpower and often lacking in protection. The Soviets put firepower first, then gave protection and mobility an equal second place. So their tanks were always equipped with good guns, had adequate protection, and were fast, if not quite as reliable as they would have liked.

Now, in the last designs of the war, each country appeared to have corrected its errors. The British, in the Centurion, at last had a powerful gun and a tank which could be relied on not to break down. With the Pershing (3), the Americans also had a powerful gun, had improved their protection, and had sufficient mobility for their needs. The Soviets had, as usual, gotten the biggest and most powerful gun inside a tank with thick armor and a reliable mechanical design.

All three, though, were little more than logical developments from what had gone before. The Centurion owed a great deal to the Comet and Cromwell which had preceded it, the Pershing to the Sherman and the M6, and the Josef Stalin to the KV-1 and the T-34. They were all the same general shape with a turret set on top to carry the gun, the engine at the rear, and a crew of driver, gunner, loader, and commander.

The war had also shown where advances in technology were needed. Efficient radio communication was a basic need, and this demanded space in the turret. Stabilization of the gun so that it would remain pointed at the target as the tank moved across country was the only way to ensure effective firing on the move. Fireproofing of the fuel and ammunition storage areas was vital, since most wartime tank losses were due to fires after being hit. And the high silhouette of some wartime designs made them easy to hit, so reducing the size of the tank became important. Just to prove that there was more than one way of making a tank, the Swedes produced the "S-Tank" in the 1950s. This had the gun rigidly fixed in the hull and had no turret. To aim the gun, the tank was swung around and the front end with the gun muzzle was lifted or lowered by altering the suspension. The design meant that the tank could be easily concealed. But it also meant that it could not fire while on the move but had to take up a position first. It was also remarkable for having two engines, a Rolls-Royce diesel for normal cruising and Boeing gas turbine, which could be coupled in, for fast acceleration. The advantage of this fixed-gun design was that the gun could be given an automatic loading mechanism, thus reducing the crew by one man and allowing the tank to be smaller. But no other country has copied the S-Tank since it is considered to be a purely defensive tank.

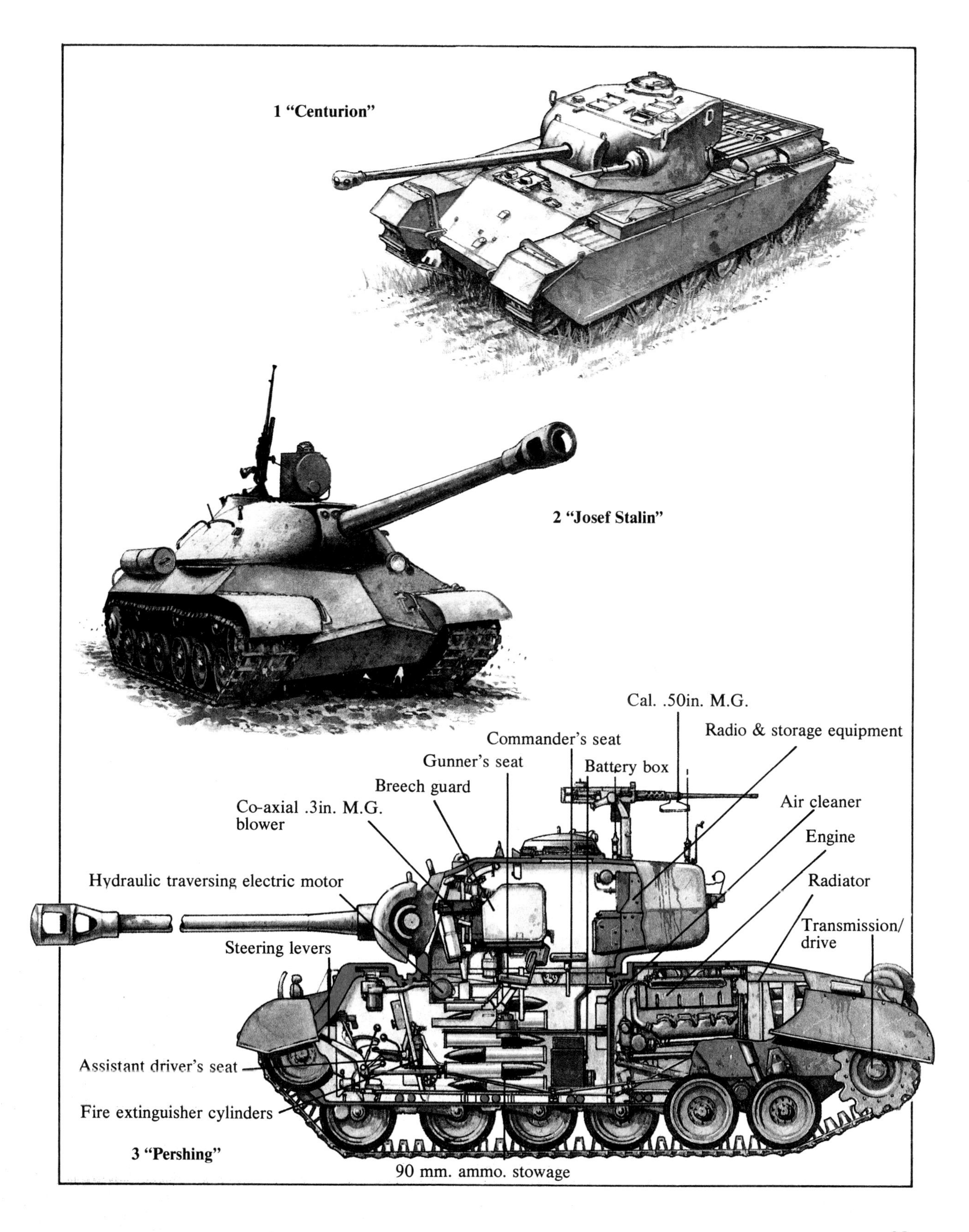
1 "Centurion"
2 "Josef Stalin"
Cal. .50in. M.G.
Radio & storage equipment
Commander's seat
Gunner's seat
Battery box
Breech guard
Co-axial .3in. M.G.
blower
Air cleaner
Engine
Hydraulic traversing electric motor
Radiator
Transmission/
drive
Steering levers
Assistant driver's seat
Fire extinguisher cylinders
3 "Pershing"
90 mm. ammo. stowage

11 Tank Destroyers

Tanks were originally intended to support the infantry so that they could reach their objective, but it soon became obvious that tanks were also the means with which to fight other tanks. Since the tanks of different armies all tended to develop along the same lines, battles between tanks were often battles between evenly-matched opponents. This led designers to think about making tanks which were intended to hunt down and destroy other tanks. To do this, they had to have good armor so that they could resist attack by enemy tanks, and an extremely powerful gun so that they could defeat any enemy tank with a single shot.

Tank destroyers were first produced by the Germans, and they came about as a by-product of another idea. German tactics demanded artillery support close to the infantry, and they developed the "assault gun," a tank body with a large artillery gun mounted instead of a turret. This could accompany the infantry and tanks making an attack and shoot directly at any fortification or resistance which was too strong to be dealt with by tanks or infantry weapons. In some battles, these assault guns shot at tanks from time to time, and from this the Germans moved to the tank destroyer idea, mounting very powerful anti-tank guns in place of the artillery pieces.

The most powerful of these was "Ferdinand" (right), a very well-armored body carrying an 88mm gun. Weighing 65 tons and with 8 inches (200mm) of armor, it was almost impossible to stop with any Allied gun, and the 88mm weapon could kill any Allied tank at long ranges. The gun was mounted in the front plate of a superstructure on top of the hull and could only swing through a small arc on each side of the center line. This proved to be its weakness. While it was deadly against any tank which it faced, a skillful enemy could creep up behind and put a shot into the much thinner armor in the rear.

The British developed a similar vehicle called "Tortoise" (top left) that weighed 78 tons, had 9 inches (228mm) of armor, and was armed with a 94mm gun. But the war was over before it was ready, and only three were ever made.

The Americans developed a much more practical vehicle, called simply the "M-10" (below left). This was a Sherman chassis with an open-topped turret carrying a powerful 90mm gun. The turret allowed all-around fire so that there was no danger of being caught from the rear. But the M-10 was not in the same class as Ferdinand or Tortoise when it came to armor or gunpower.

The first British tank destroyer was called "Archer" and used the body of the old Valentine tank. On top of this was an armored box into which a 17-pounder (76mm) gun was mounted. But the only way it could be made to fit was by pointing it over the back of the body. So Archer had to reverse into position instead of driving forward in the usual way. The other problem was that space was so tight the driver had to get out of his seat quickly as soon as he stopped. Otherwise, the gun would hit his head when it recoiled after firing.

Ferdinand

12 The Next Generation

In the Korean War of 1950-53, the North Korean and Chinese armies were provided with Russian T-34s, the Americans used Shermans, and the British, their Centurions. That the American and Russian designs were rather old was made evident by the superiority of the Centurion, so in both countries new designs were put in hand.

The first Soviet product was the T-54, an improved T-34 with better armor, a new turret, and a powerful 100mm gun. This was followed by the PT-76, an amphibious tank mounted with a 76mm gun, which could swim at about 6 mph (10 km/h). Then in 1957 the West saw the first T-10 heavy tank, an improved Josef Stalin with a new 122mm gun.

The Americans began by building the M41 "Walker Bulldog" armed with a new 76mm gun. At 23 tons, this was a curious vehicle since it was too big for a light tank and too small for a medium one. It was too heavy for airborne operations, and the gun was not powerful enough to deal with enemy tanks. Work then began on improving the M26, by fitting it with new engines and calling it the M46 "Patton." Then they developed a new turret with a better 90mm gun, fitted that to the M46, and called it the M47 "Patton."

Below: A British "Chieftain" main battle tank with 120mm gun. The commander is in his hatch, with machine gun on one side and searchlight on the other. The driver is also visible. In action both would be concealed, using periscopes for viewing.

The British developed "Chieftain" to replace the Centurion (left). This was the most formidable tank in the world when it appeared in 1965. It had an extremely powerful 120mm gun, good armor protection, and excellent mobility.

The Americans developed a 152mm weapon that could be used either as a gun or as a missile launcher. The tank was the "Sheridan," a light, fast vehicle capable of being lifted in an aircraft but with a powerful punch to deal with other tanks. Unfortunately, it had many mechanical defects so the US Army went back to the conventional design and produced the M60, an improved "Patton" with a 105mm gun borrowed from the British.

Below: A collection of battle tanks. An American M551 Sheridan is about to pass a Soviet T54. Behind the T54 is an American M47, and behind the Sheridan is an American M60A3.

The Americans used the M47, Sheridan, and M60 in Vietnam, while the Vietnamese used the Soviet T-54s. American and Soviet tanks also faced each other in the various battles between Israeli and Arab armies, while British, American, and Soviet tanks found themselves on different sides in the India-Pakistan war.

Several countries began building tanks in the 1950s, among them France, which developed an unusual design known as the AMX-13. This had its gun rigidly fixed in the turret so that it could only be elevated by tilting the whole turret. This was done so that an automatic loading mechanism could be used, thus reducing the turret crew to two men, the commander and gun aimer. As soon as the gun had fired, it automatically threw out the empty cartridge case and reloaded. This system has since been adopted by other countries, but the French were the first to make it work reliably, and the AMX-13 was sold to armies all round the world.

13 The Armament

To destroy tanks, a gun must be very powerful and accurate. This generally means a long and heavy gun. To support the infantry, a gun needs only to be accurate. Since the damage will be done by the explosive inside the shell, it can be short and light.

Conventional guns, the sort used since tanks began, are rifled. They have spiral grooves in the barrel so that the shell spins as it is fired, and it is this spinning which keeps it accurately on course. The shell is shot out by exploding a propelling charge of powder behind it, and this charge can be loaded into the gun either in a metal cartridge case or in a cloth or plastic bag. The cartridge case also acts as a seal at the breech end of the gun, which is opened and closed to load, so that all the gas made by the explosion pushes the shell and none leaks out into the tank. The "bag-charge" gun (used in the Chieftain, for example) needs a more complicated breech closing system to prevent any leak of gas.

To simply smash a hole in armor plate, all that is needed is a heavy steel shot with a point on it. No explosive is required. For infantry support and for attacking buildings and troops in the open, a high explosive shell is used. This is a hollow steel shell filled with explosive and with a fuse in the nose which will detonate the explosive as soon as it hits the target.

The latest development in tank guns, first introduced by the Russians, is a smooth-bored gun which fires a shell or shot with fins which keep it flying in the right direction. Without the rifling, the shot can be fired out at a higher speed so that it has more smashing power at the target. Indeed it strikes with such force that ordinary steel shot will shatter, and it is now usual to make the shot of a

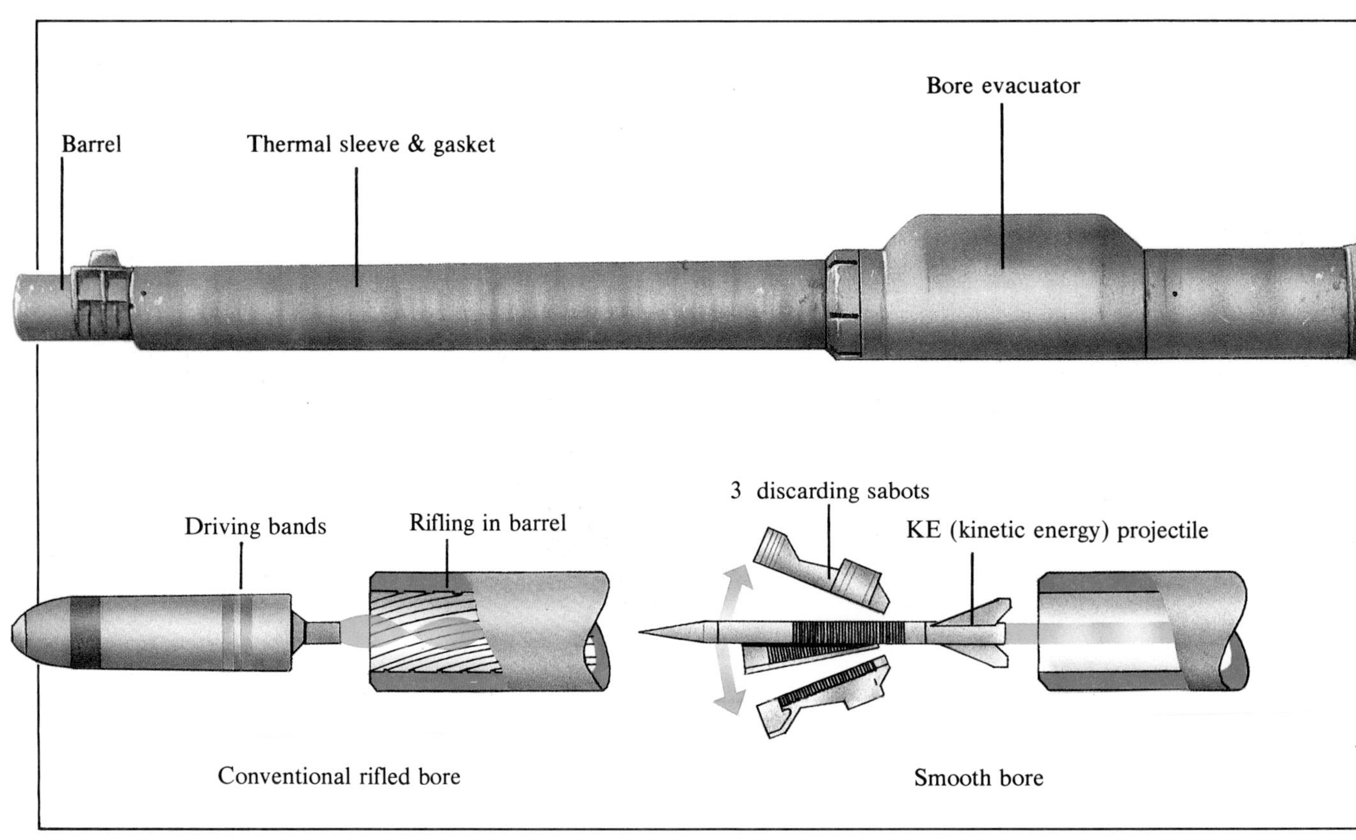

very heavy material such as tungsten or uranium which resists shatter and delivers a more powerful blow because it is heavier than steel.

For lighter guns, there are special "High Explosive Anti-Tank" (HEAT) shells which rely upon having the explosive formed into a hollow cone with a thin metal lining. When this shell detonates outside the tank, the cone focuses the explosive force into a very fine jet which blasts through the armor and sprays molten metal and flame inside the tank.

The most powerful anti-tank shot is the "Discarding Sabot" shot designed by the British in 1943 and since widely adopted. It consists of a hard core of tungsten metal surrounded by a "sabot" or shoe of light metal that brings it up to the full diameter of the gun barrel. On firing, the shot passes down the gun barrel at very high speed, and, as soon as it leaves the barrel, the "sabot" splits apart and falls away, leaving the core to go to the target. The same principle is now used with smoothbore guns, firing fin-stabilized shot. It allows the penetrative core to be long, heavy, and thin, the best shape for piercing armor.

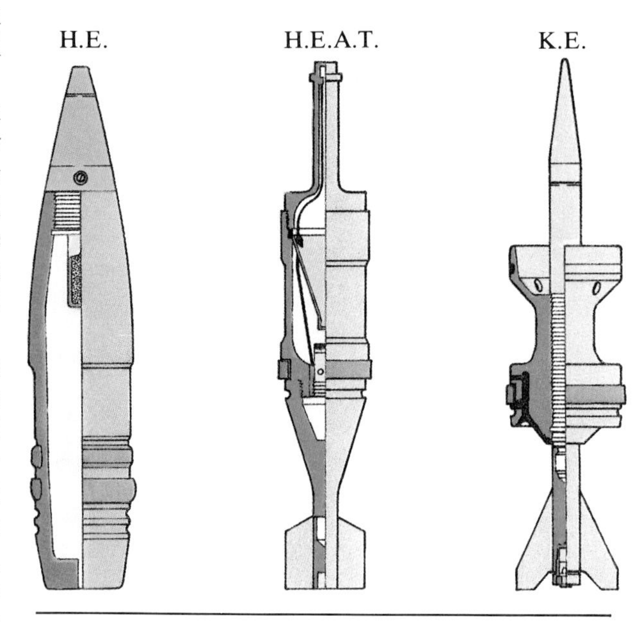

Above: The three basic types of ammunition used by tanks: (left) the anti-personnel high explosive shell; (center) the hollow charge shell; (right) the fin-stabilized discarding sabot shot.

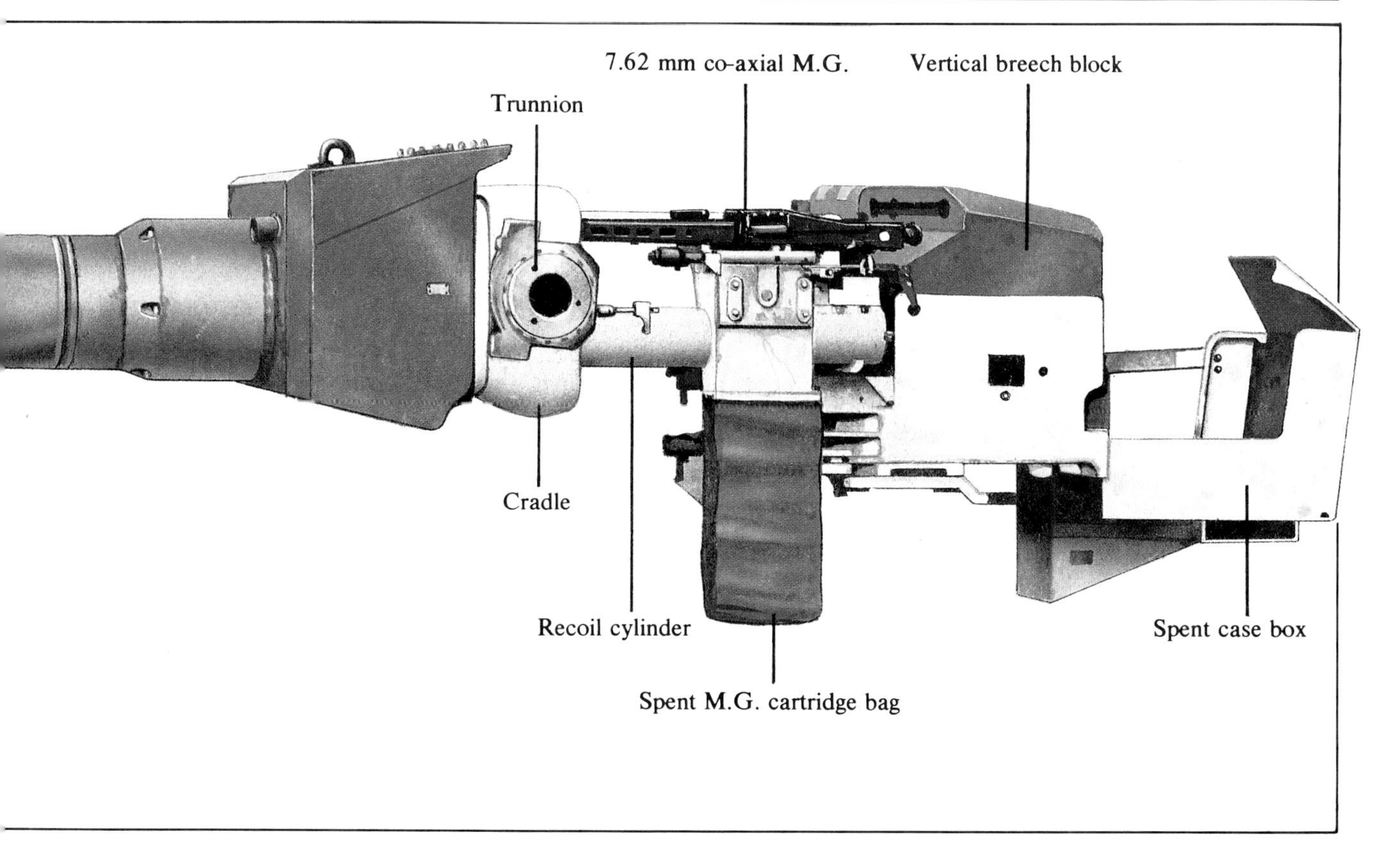

14 Driving the Tank

The earliest tanks dragged a pair of huge wheels behind them and swiveled these by means of steel ropes in order to change direction. It was not a very good system and was soon abandoned for "track steering" in which one track was slowed down or stopped while the other kept going or was speeded up so that it swerved around in the direction of the slower track. Various ideas have been tried, but this is still the basic principle behind steering a tank.

The engine drives the tracks through a complicated system of gears known as the "transmission" — just like the gearbox of an ordinary car. The transmission also acts as the steering system being connected to the controls so that it slows down or speeds up the tracks as required. The transmission drives two toothed wheels, known as the "driving sprockets," which connect with the track and force it around the remaining wheels, which support the tank on the track. They are sprung so that they can move up and down to smooth out the travel across rough ground and they have solid rubber tires to absorb the roughness and make life more comfortable for the crew.

The engine is usually at the rear of the tank so as to leave the forward part for the fighting compartment. The driver sits right at the front where he can obtain the best view. In front of the driver are his controls, which are usually fairly simple and can be compared with those of a car. There is the steering control, which may be a wheel but is more likely to be a simple handlebar or a pair of levers, one for each track. There is a gear lever, a clutch, a brake pedal, and an accelerator or throttle. Due to the great weight of the tank and the distance between the driver and the engine and transmission, most of the controls on a modern tank are power-assisted, and many now have automatic transmissions so the driver has no need to change gear.

The engine is started in the usual way and allowed to warm up for a few minutes. Then the driver pushes in his clutch and engages first gear or selects "Drive" in his automatic transmission.

To steer, he moves the wheel or handlebar or pulls on the track "tiller" lever in the direction in which he wishes to move. The track on that side slows down, the other track speeds up, and the tank swings its nose across until the driver releases the

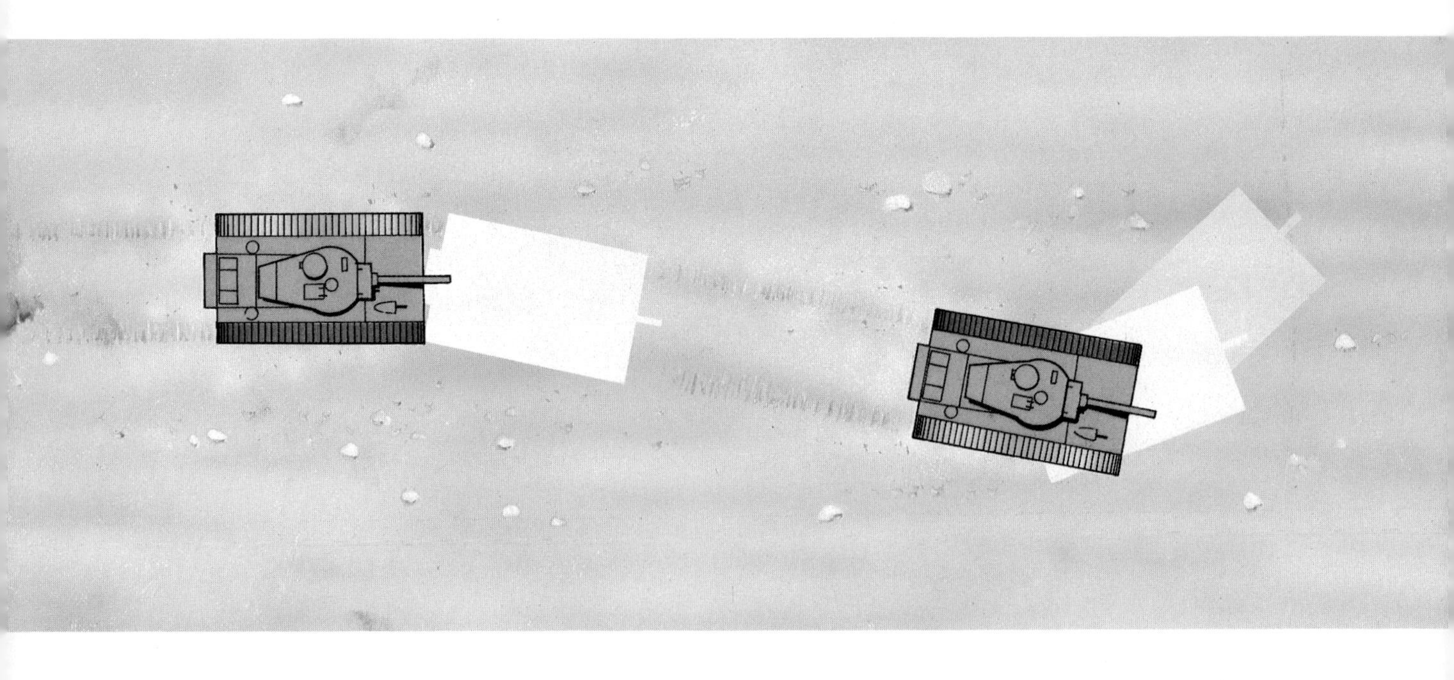

lever or control. As he speeds up, so he will select a higher gear or the automatic gearbox will select one for him.

Although the driver can see where he is going, sitting up with his head through a hatch in the armor, this is only done when the tank is not in action. Then he lowers his seat and closes the hatch, leaving him a periscope through which to see ahead. This restricts his vision, and he now relies very much on the tank commander to warn him of obstacles and tell him which direction to go and how fast. To simply drive a tank is not very difficult. But to operate one in combat conditions over rough country with a limited view and with the instructions of the commander the only guide, takes a very great amount of skill.

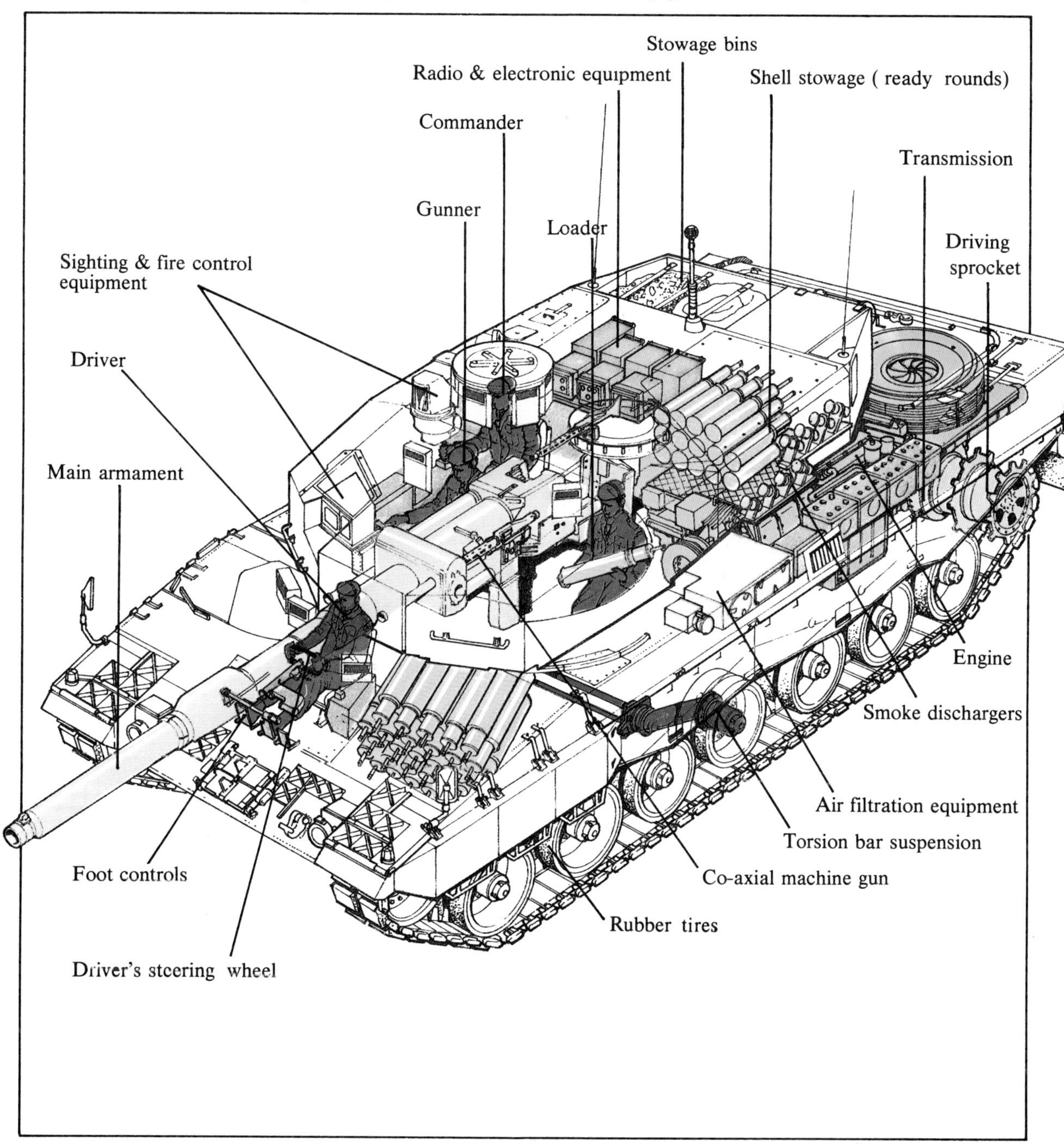

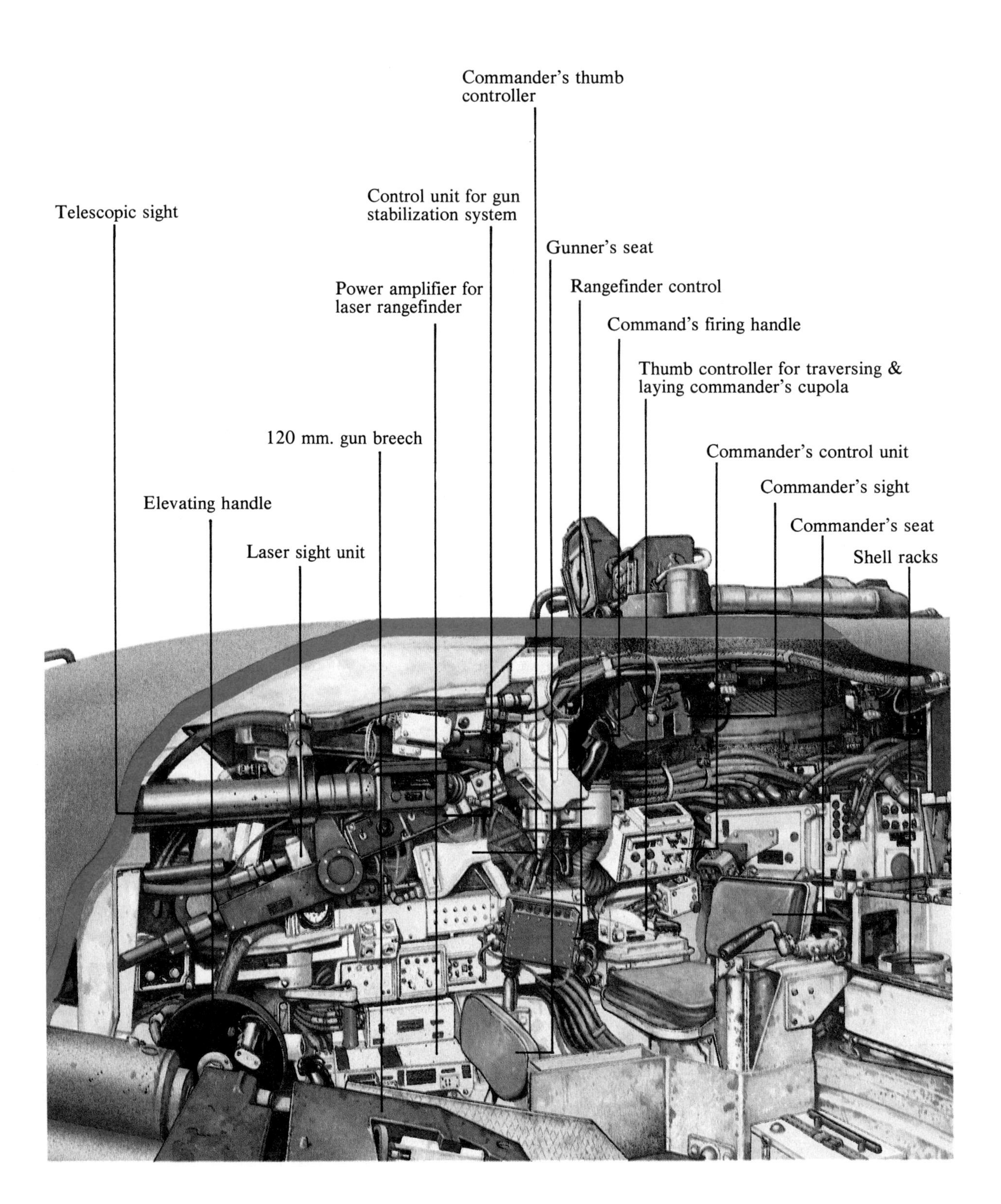
Commander's thumb controller
Telescopic sight
Control unit for gun stabilization system
Gunner's seat
Rangefinder control
Power amplifier for laser rangefinder
Command's firing handle
Thumb controller for traversing & laying commander's cupola
120 mm. gun breech
Commander's control unit
Commander's sight
Elevating handle
Commander's seat
Laser sight unit
Shell racks

15 Commanding the Tank

The commander of the tank has many responsibilities. He must read his map and direct the driver, watch all around for enemy action, keep in touch with his own commander, keep in touch with other tanks of his group, direct the gunner to fire at various targets, and keep a check on ammunition and fuel, and, above all, keep his mind on whatever task he has been given, whether conducting an attack, supporting infantry, or merely looking for information.

To do all this, he has much equipment inside the turret and is assisted by the gunner and loader, who also operate inside the turret. The gunner sits on the left of the gun with his sights, the loader sits on the right, and the commander sits behind and above him, where he can see through his hatch. This hatch carries nine observation periscopes and a sighting periscope so that he has all-around vision and can also aim the gun by overriding the controls if he sees a target. It is quicker for him to swing the gun around by using his override than attempt to describe the target to the gunner. Alongside the hatch is a small infrared searchlight that allows him to see in the dark and a machine gun that is linked to the light to shoot at anything the searchlight picks up. The loader has another hatch and a single periscope which he can swing around to scan in all directions. The three men agree on how to watch all around — the commander looks in one direction, the loader in another, and the gunner in a third so that the whole area around the tank is constantly watched.

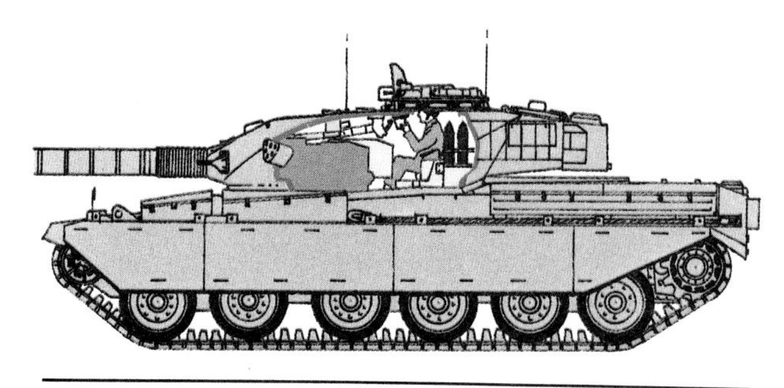

Above: The commander's position in the tank. Left: A view of the turret. The commander's seat is at the right with the gunner in front and below. Notice the great amount of electronic equipment inside a modern tank.

Some tanks allow the commander to fire the gun in cases where this might be faster than trying to put the gunner on to the target. This is now made easier by using TV-type viewers, which allow the commander to see the picture in the gunner's sight, and computers, which make all the necessary corrections for shooting at a moving target.

To talk to the other members of the crew, there is an "intercom" telephone. Everyone wears headphones and a microphone and can talk to each other freely. At the same time, the commander and loader can switch their headsets to the radio network to send or receive messages from other tanks or from the higher commander.

On the left side of the turret in an armored cover, is a second more powerful searchlight that can emit white light or infrared light. This is connected in sympathy with the main gun and can illuminate targets up to a mile away.

There have been many ideas for labor-saving devices, usually in order to reduce the number of crew men and thus make the tank less crowded. We have already discussed automatic loading mechanisms as one method of saving manpower. Some years ago, the Soviets decided to fit an automatic cartridge-case ejector that, after the gun fired, pulled the hot case from the breech and threw it through a little hatch in the back of the turret. Unfortunately, it often got out of adjustment, and the empty case missed the hole, bouncing around the turret, damaging equipment, and injuring the gunner and loader.

An idea being tried by some armies today is an electronic position-finding system. Controlled by a gyro-compass and the tank's speedometer, it has a known position set in at the start of the day. After that, it keeps continuous record of the tank's movement and location, relieving the commander of the need to constantly read his map.

16 Taking the Infantry Along

The whole reason for inventing the tank was to help the infantry to reach their objective through barbed wire and machine gun fire, and this requirement still applies. The early tanks moved at a walking pace so that infantry on foot could walk behind them. But as tanks improved their speed, it became necessary to put the infantry into vehicles to travel with them. At first, ordinary trucks were used. But during the Second World War, the German army developed armored carriers that gave the infantry protection from bullets and shell splinters as they followed the tanks. Once the tanks ran into some opposition, the infantry carriers would stop, and the men would get out and go into action.

In some cases, however, the Germans found that stopping the carriers and disembarking the men was dangerous. Instead they could be very effective if they stayed in the carriers, firing their rifles through hatches, as the carrier drove forward with the tanks towards the enemy position.

In northern France, the British army was confronted with the problem of attacking a very strong German position. They decided the only way was to put the infantry into armored vehicles and drive them through the German infantry defenses to attack the rear line of anti-tank guns, knocking these out and making the attack safe for the tanks. To do this, they took a number of old tanks, removed the turrets, and packed the infantry into them. The plan worked well and these "Armored Personnel Carriers" (or APCs as they came to be known) were used in several operations, saving many lives in the process.

After the war, there was a great deal of debate about APCs, but eventually most armies adopted them. The principal question was whether they were to be regarded simply as "battle taxis" that took the infantry to where they had to fight and dropped them or whether they could become fighting vehicles of some sort which could help the infantry. Most people settled for "battle taxis," and the most common of these is probably the American M113. This was simply an armored box on tracks that can carry 11 infantrymen as well as the driver and the vehicle commander.

In more recent years, the "MICV" or "Mechanized Infantry Combat Vehicle" has gained in popularity. This is an APC that carries its own armament — usually a fast-firing 20 to 30mm cannon in the turret, some machine guns, possibly an anti-tank guided missile as well — and has room for a squad of infantrymen with their equipment. The American "M2 Bradley" is one example, and the British "MCV-80" another. These both have cannon mounted in their turrets, while the infantrymen carry their own anti-tank weapons. The Soviets use the "BMP" (Boevaya Mashina Pekhotz or Infantry Fighting Machine), which has a crew of three and carries eight infantrymen. It is armed with a 73mm gun and also carries a "Sagger" anti-tank missile on a rail over the gun barrel.

There is still a good deal of debate going on about the best size of squad or the best armament. It will be some years before this is settled since none of these MICVs has yet been used in combat.

The newest idea on taking the infantry along has been the Israeli "Merkava" (Chariot) tank. This has the engine and the transmission at the front and has a door in the rear leading into the large fighting compartment. Into this space, four infantrymen can climb and ride with the tank and leap out and go into action when the tank commander needs them. Alternatively, the space can be used for carrying wounded men off the battlefield.

Right: Some modern armored vehicles for infantry: (top) the American M2 Bradley carries a 3-man crew and 6 infantry and is armed with a 25mm cannon. Below it, the M113 APC carries a 2-man crew and 11 infantry. Note the firing ports in the body for the infantry to fire from when moving. The Soviet BMP-1 is armed with a 73mm gun and an anti-tank missile above it and carries a 3-man crew and 8 infantrymen. (bottom): The British MCV-80 has a two-man crew and carries 8 infantrymen. It is armed with a 30mm Rarden cannon and is driven by a Rolls-Royce engine.

M2 Bradley
M113 APC
BMP-1
MCV-80

17 Tanks for Special Tasks

There are jobs which require special types of tank, some of which are not equipped for fighting. When an armored column advances, it requires technical assistance of various sorts. These jobs are best done by vehicles capable of traveling with the tanks, which are armored to protect them and their crews and can operate over the roughest ground.

One of the biggest problems facing tanks in the advance is crossing rivers or ditches that are too big for the tank to cross unaided. For this purpose, the bridging tank is used (below). This uses a tank body and tracks but carries a folded bridge on top. When required, the tank is maneuvered into position on the bank of the river or ditch. The bridge is slowly unfolded from its stored position and extended in front of the tank and then lowered until the end rests on the other side of the obstacle. The bridge is unhooked from the tank which then backs away so the combat tanks can cross. Later, when a more permanent bridge has been built or a nearby bridge has been captured, the bridging tank can return, connect up to the bridge, lift it and fold it back in place, and then go on to rejoin the combat tanks and be ready for the next obstacle.

Any tank can break down or be hit by a shell or run over a mine. Provided the damage is not too severe and the tank is worth repairing, it can be hauled away to safety to be mended. To do this, "recovery tanks" are built (below right). They have

Below: A diagram showing how the bridging tank unfolds the bridge and projects it forward over a river or ditch.

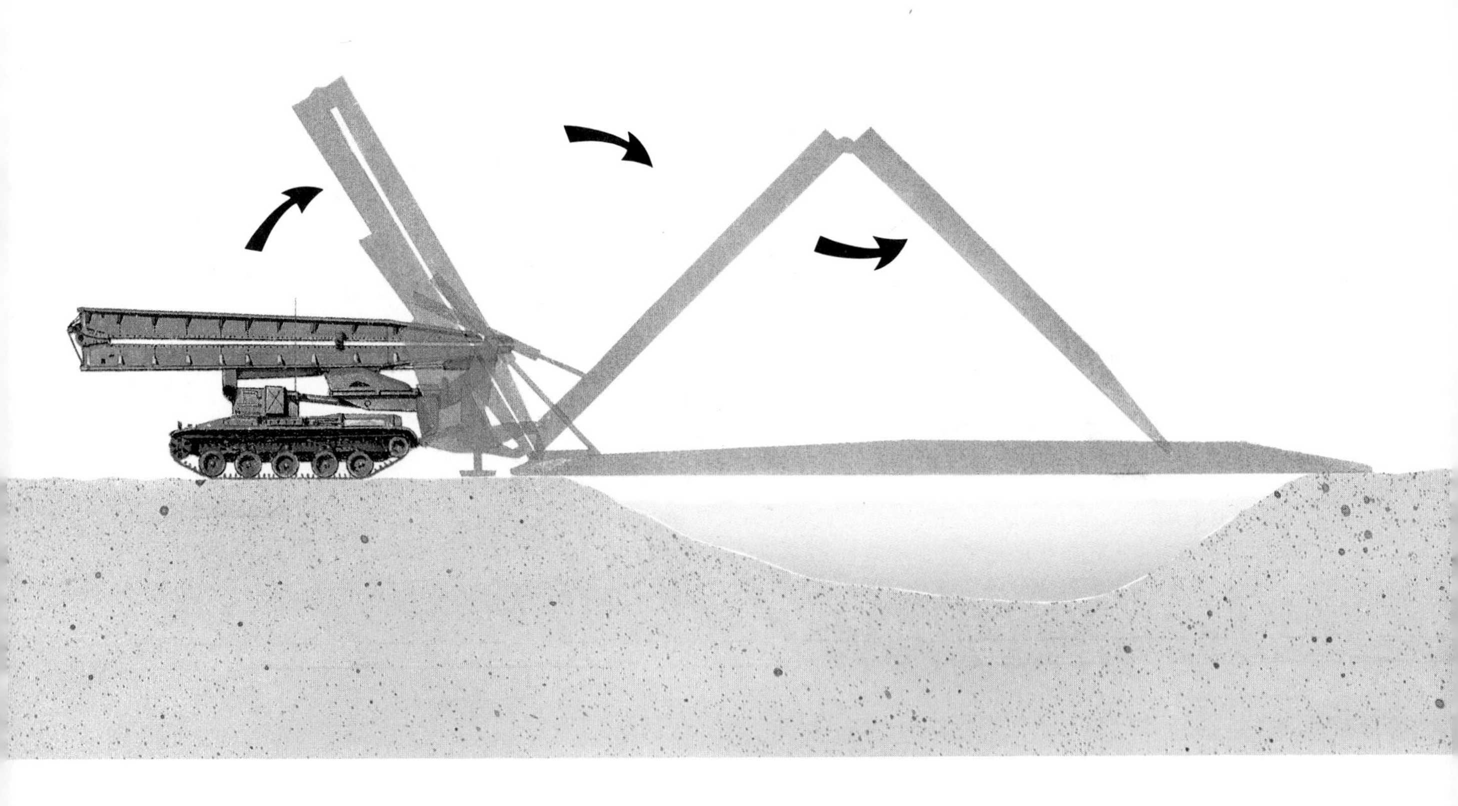

a normal tank body but are fitted with powerful winches and cranes so that they can hook on to the damaged tank and drag it clear or perhaps tow it away or haul it on to a transporter or use the crane to remove damaged parts and insert new ones.

The "flail" tanks, which were developed for the invasion of Europe in 1944, are no longer used. Instead, several countries have developed mine-clearing tanks that push a heavy roller or set of rollers ahead so that any mine will be detonated by the weight of the roller. Opinions on the value of these tanks are mixed. It is not very difficult for the mine designer to invent fuses which will refuse to function at the first or second pressure of the rollers but will detonate as the weight of the tank comes on to it.

Tanks usually have thinner armor on top than on the front and sides, and today it is becoming more common to use helicopters with missiles or cannon to attack tanks from the air. As a result, anti-aircraft tanks are now being developed. The German army uses "Gepard" (above right), which carries two 35mm cannon and radar, while the American army has "Sergeant York" carrying two 40mm cannon and radar. These vehicles are built on the standard tank chassis and can travel along with the armored column keeping watch on the air. They can open fire while moving and have a high probability of being able to shoot down aircraft before they can get close enough to threaten the tanks.

Tank transporters are special heavy truck-and-trailer combinations used to move tanks over long distances. A tank uses a great deal of fuel — as much as 1 gallon for every mile it travels — and its tracks wear out quickly, especially when driving on roads. So if it is necessary to move tanks over a long distance outside the combat zone, they are loaded on to transporters. For very long distances, they can often be moved by railway, but this is not always convenient. Railway movement often places restrictions on the size of the tank so it can pass under bridges and between platforms.

Above: The German "Gepard" anti-aircraft tank

Below: A recovery tank for the rescue of damaged vehicles

18 Today's Main Battle Tanks

T-72 (top left). This is the latest Soviet tank known in any detail to the West, though there are rumors of a newer model called the T-80. The T-72 was first seen in 1977 and is really the latest step in a long line of development which goes back to the T-34 of wartime years. The engine is thought to be a 750 horsepower diesel, which will move the 38-tonner along at 48 mph (80 km/h). The main armament is a 125mm smoothbore gun, said to be able to pierce 12 inches (300mm) of armor at 3,300 feet (1000m).

Challenger (center left). This will replace some of the Chieftain tanks in British service during the 1980s. It is really an improved Chieftain, using the same 120mm gun but with a new kind of armor known as "Chobham" armor after the place in which it was invented. Instead of plain steel, Chobham armor uses layers of steel and other materials so that it can resist attack by both shot and shell. Another improvement is the use of a new Rolls-Royce engine of 1200 horsepower, giving the 62-ton Challenger a speed of 36 mph (60 km/h).

Leopard (bottom left). The Leopard became the West German army's main battle tank in 1963. Then the Germans went on to develop Leopard 2, first issued in late 1978. Leopard 2 uses a combination of ordinary armor and Chobham armor to give good protection. It is armed with a powerful 120mm smoothbore gun for firepower and has a 1500 horsepower turbo-charged diesel engine, which drives the 55-tonner at 43 mph (72 km/h). The West German army have placed orders for 1800 Leopard 2 tanks, and the Netherlands army have ordered another 445 to replace their Centurions.

Chieftain (top right). This is the British army's principal tank that first appeared in 1961. About 900 were made for British use, and it has also been sold to Iran, Jordan, and Kuwait. The main armament is a 120mm rifled gun that fires with great accuracy. There are infrared units that permit the driver and the gunner to see in the dark, and there is a computer coupled to a laser that measures the target range and calculates exactly how much to aim away in order to hit a moving target. Once the gunner has pointed his gun at the target, a stabilizer will keep it correctly aimed no matter how the tank moves. The engine produces 750 horsepower and can drive the Chieftain at 29 mph (48 km/h) on roads.

Abrams (center right). This is the latest American tank. First built in 1980, it is thought that some 7,000 of them will be in service by 1990. Like Challenger, Abrams has Chobham armor for greater protection but uses a 105mm gun. It is planned to fit it with a 120mm gun in the future to give greater firepower. The engine is a gas turbine that produces 1500 horsepower and can drive the 54-tonne tank at 43 mph (72 km/h). The driver is in a reclining seat in the front center, and the commander, gunner, and loader work in the large turret.

AMX-32 (bottom right). This has been developed in France but will not equip the French army as it is being offered for export sale instead. It carries a 105mm gun but can be fitted with the German 102mm smoothbore if preferred. There is the usual four-man crew, and a 700 horsepower engine drives the 38 tonner at 39 mph (65 km/h). The armor is of plain cast steel, and the AMX-32 is unusual in having a fast-firing 20mm cannon alongside the main gun, probably intended for dealing with light targets which do not require the enormous power of the main armament.

19 Modern Tank Tactics

The battlefield of today has changed a good deal from that of Colonel Swinton, and his simple tactics of crushing the wire and sweeping up the trench line are no longer of much use. In the years since then, many tactical theories have been tried out — from having single tanks attempting cavalry-like raids to having squadrons of tanks imitating naval tactics and maneuvering like fleets of ships across the desert. Since the principal enemy of the tank is not another tank but an anti-tank weapon, most tactics are based on avoiding anti-tank weapons.

Ever since tanks first appeared, they have usually operated in conjunction with infantry. It has often been thought that the tanks would be better off by themselves, but history disproves this. It is a confirmed fact that whenever a force of tanks and infantry has been separated, either by chance or by a skillful enemy, the enemy is then able to select one of the two groups and defeat it at leisure.

The first tactical rule then is that the tanks and the infantry must work in cooperation, and this is the reason for the development of APCs, which allow the infantry to keep close to the tanks at all times. But how can infantry "protect" such a well-protected thing as a heavily armored and well-armed tank?

Tanks advance in small groups of three or four, each watching all around to be able to warn the others of any danger. They do not normally charge across country in full view but move in short dashes between selected spots where they can conceal themselves. Thus the first tank of a group will go forward to a selected clump of trees. Once there, the tank crew will observe the front for danger while the second tank comes up, passes it, and hides behind a barn. The third and fourth will come up and conceal themselves, say, in a sunken road or behind a rise in the ground where the commander can see from his hatch on the turret but which conceals the body of the tank. With all concealed and watching, the first tank now moves off to another hide, and so on.

The modern tank is provided with an impressive collection of sensing devices to aid the crew in watching for trouble. Electronic night vision equipment permits seeing in the dark or in poor visibility, short-range radar can detect movement, and detectors will warn the crew if laser beams or shots are aimed in their direction and indicate the source. Infrared viewers can "see" tanks or men hidden behind natural cover or camouflage and can detect missiles being fired.

If, during these moves, one tank crew sees trouble ahead — perhaps another tank or an anti-tank weapon hidden in wait — then one or two of the tanks can try to move around and take the enemy from the rear or side while his attention is fixed on his front. But if the obstacle looks too big — it may be an infantry company position with several anti-tank weapons, mortars, machine guns — then the infantry in their APCs are called up. The tanks will take up positions "hull down" behind cover where most of the tank is concealed but over which the gun can fire and begin bombarding the position. The infantry will dismount, work their way to one side, and begin an attack on foot. While the infantry keep the enemy occupied, the tanks can move around and add their weight to the attack from a different direction. The infantrymen can engage the anti-tank weapons with machine gun and mortar fire, so that attention is distracted from the tanks. And the tanks can bombard the enemy machine guns and mortars so that they cannot harm the infantry.

At the present time, there is much discussion over the tactics which will be necessary to defend tanks against a new threat, the helicopter. Most armies have now developed armored helicopters carrying missiles, and these can be very difficult for tanks to spot since the crew are generally concerned with watching all around them at ground level. The anti-tank missile fired by infantrymen is also a problem, but experience in the Arab-Israeli wars suggests that machine gun fire by tanks against any suspicious area might be sufficient to put the operator of the missile off his aim.

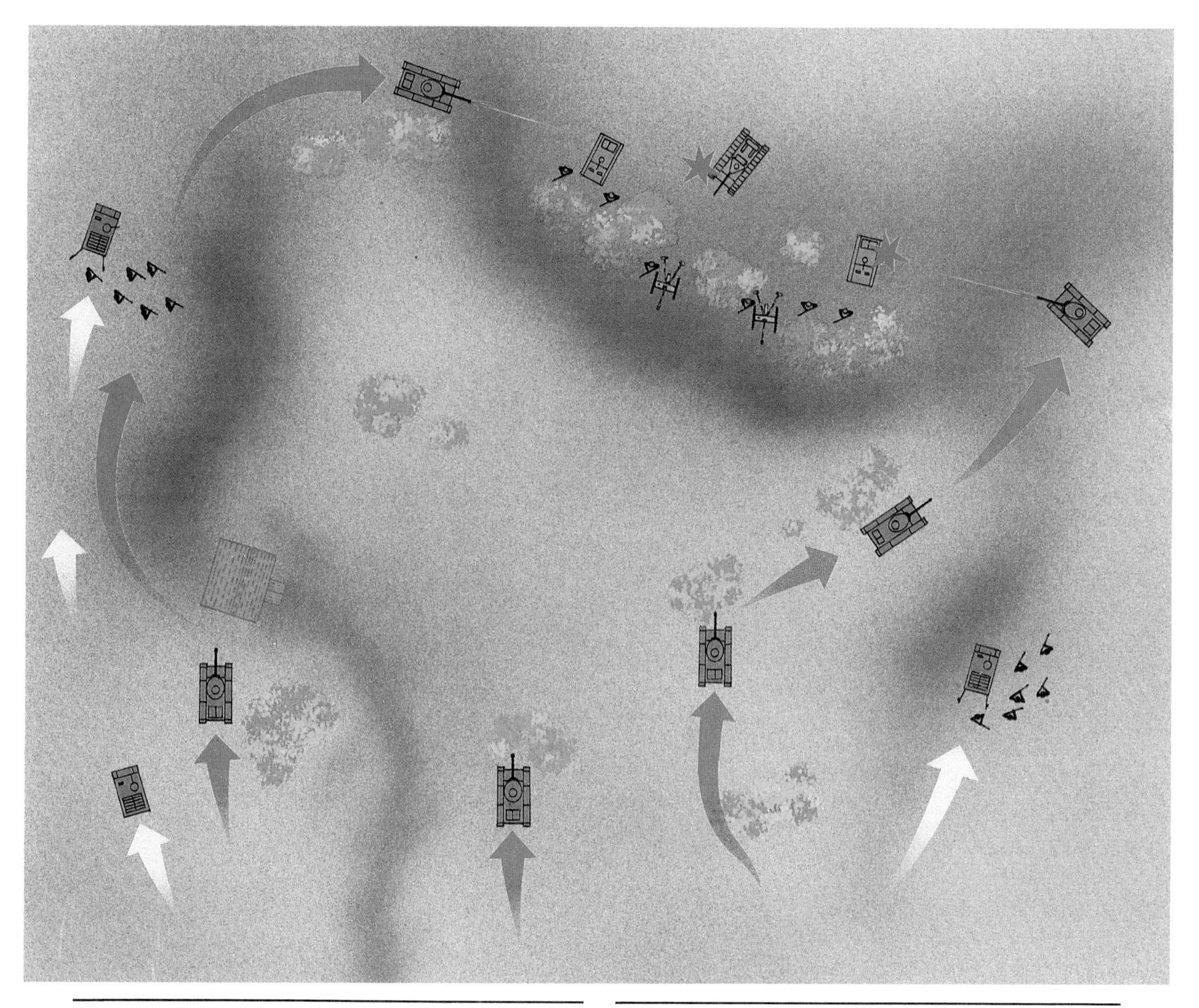

Above: A simple tactical operation carried out by a troop of tanks. On approaching the enemy position (behind the trees, top), one tank takes up a hull-down firing position (bottom center) and draws the attention of the enemy. One tank, accompanied by infantry in an IFV, moves around a flank (left), first using a convenient house to conceal his movement. The infantry disembark and take up firing positions while the tank moves further around. At the same time, two more tanks with another IFV and infantry move to the other flank (right) using trees and other natural features to conceal their movement. The infantry leave their IFV and take up a position from which they can fire and also prepare to move in to occupy the position when it is taken. Finally the tanks, using as much cover as they can find and coordinating their movements by radio messages, move together from both flanks to make the final assault. One tank deals with the enemy tank while the others pick off the IFVs and guns. Once this has been done, the infantry will get into their IFVs and motor on to the objective to place it in a state of defense. The tanks will take up defensive positions facing the direction of the advance, and support troops will move up, pass through the new position, and continue the attack.

20 Tomorrow's Tank

Survivability is an important feature in the design of tanks being prepared as replacements for the present tanks in about the year 2000.

The most prominent feature of most tanks is the turret. Even when the tank is "hull-down" — with the body concealed behind a rise in the ground and only the turret and gun showing — it is still a fairly prominent object and a good target. One suggestion is to do away with the turret, put everybody inside the body of the tank,and mount the gun by itself in an armored casing on the roof of the tank. It would be guided and operated by remote control and loaded by an automatic unit. As a result, a hull-down tank would show only the gun over the crest — a tiny target, probably no more than $1\frac{1}{2}$ feet square, which would be difficult to see and extremely difficult to hit. Other advantages would be that with the gun breech removed from inside, the tank could be narrower and also lower because the traditional two-level arrangement (with the commander and gunner higher than the driver) would be abandoned for one-level, reducing the height of the tank by about one-third. This means that more armor could be used to give better protection since the area to be armored would be less.

A recent Swedish design, UDES-17, is a low-silhouette tank with the gun fitted so that it forms part of the tank. It can be raised above the tank and rotated when necessary to fire over cover. The US Army is experimenting with the "HSTV" (High Survivability Test Vehicle) (top right). This is a low-slung tank with a very flat turret which has the gun in the center, the commander on one side, and the automatic loading machinery on the other side. The gunner and the driver lie in the hull, both with similar controls and with the gun control equipment mounted between them so that either of them can drive or operate the gun, which is a high-velocity 75mm weapon. The whole vehicle weighs just over 18 tons, has a 750 horsepower engine, and can move at 48 mph (80 km/h).

Another Swedish design being tested is UDES-XX-20 (below right), which consists of two separate units connected together. The rear unit contains the engine, a transmission, and a track suspension and drives the front unit which also has its own tracks and transmission. The crew and gun are in the front unit. This "articulated" design gives great maneuverability — UDES-XX-20 has recorded speeds of over 36 mph (60 km/h) when operating in deep snow conditions — and with the gun mounted above the front unit in a remote-control pod, the whole vehicle is very low and easily hidden. UDES-XX-20 is being studied as a possible tank destroyer, an interesting comeback of an idea which has been almost entirely ignored for the past 30 years.

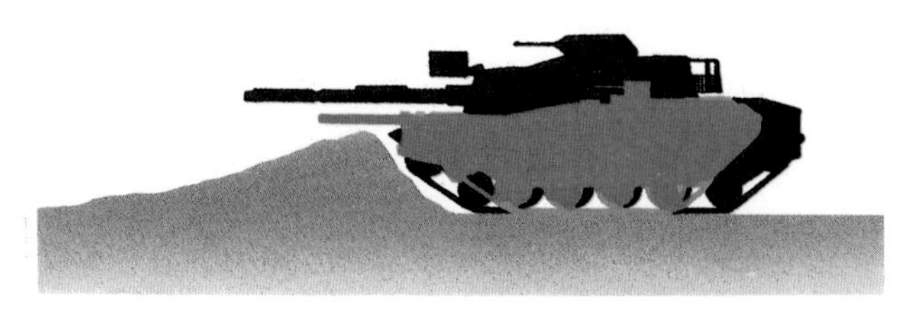

Above: A comparison between a conventional turretted tank and (in front) a Swedish S-tank, showing how little of the latter can be seen in a "hull-down" firing position

Not all new ideas work well. In developing a new design of medium tank in the 1970s, the US Army decided to save space by putting the driver in the turret, and connecting his controls by electronic cables. His seat was also electronically controlled so that no matter where the turret went, the driver still faced forward. On paper it was a good idea, but in practice it was found that after half an hour, the poor driver didn't know which direction he was facing or where the tank was going.

Below: Two possible solutions to the question of survivability on the battlefield; (top) the experimental American High Survivability Test Vehicle which has the driver and gunner semi-reclining in the hull and the commander seated in the hull but with his head in the turret. The gun is automatically loaded and remotely controlled by either the gunner or the driver, and the commander has remote control for the machine gun on top of the turret. At the bottom is the Swedish UDES-XX-20 articulated tank. It is in two units connected by hydraulic steering rams; the rear unit contains the engine and fuel, while the front unit contains the crew and has the gun remotely mounted on top. There is a connection between the units which allows the engine to drive the tracks of both units, and steering is done partly by braking the tracks and partly by bending the two units by using the hydraulic rams. Because of the central connection the whole assembly clings closely to the ground when crossing rough country and is very difficult to detect. The double track unit spreads the weight and power over the ground so that it has excellent grip and can also drive across mud and snow which would not support a more compact vehicle which placed a heavier load on its wheels or tracks. This design, with the gun pod-mounted also means that the armament can be changed easily without major alteration to the rest of the tank.

Glossary

AFV
Armored Fighting Vehicle. Military term covering all armored combat equipment — tanks, APCs, IFVs, armored cars, etc.
AMPHIBIOUS
Capable of operating on land or in water without special preparations
APC
Armored Personnel Carrier. Armored vehicle for transport of infantry. May be lightly armed
APPLIQUE ARMOR
Additional armor which can be attached to a tank or other vehicle to give greater protection than the basic armor
ARMOR
The protective plating around an AFV. Can be of three kinds: *Homogeneous* is of the same resistance all the way through; *Face-hardened* has the outer surface extremely hard, the remainder less hard but also less brittle; and *Laminated,* which is made up of several thicknesses of different materials — steel, titanium, ceramics — to defeat different types of attack weapon
ARMORED CAR
Light, wheeled, armored vehicle used for scouting and reconnaissance
ARV
Armored Recovery Vehicle. Special tank, without gun but with cranes, winches, ground anchors, and other equipment that enables it to rescue and tow away damaged tanks
ASSAULT GUN
Self-propelled artillery weapon that is designed to accompany tanks in the assault and give heavy gun support at short range
BARBETTE
Gun mounting allowing only limited traverse; usually applied to a mounting in the side-wall of a tank
BASKET
Structure which hangs down below the turret, inside the hull. The turret crew, gun, ammunition, radio, etc., are all carried in the basket so that they all revolve with the turret
BOGIES
Small roadwheels supporting the weight of the tank or vehicle
BUSTLE
The overhanging rear section of a tank turret, usually containing radio equipment or ammunition
CANNON
An automatic gun of caliber between 20mm and 30mm; used as main armament of IFVs and secondary armament of some tanks
CO-AXIAL
On the same axis; used when speaking of tank machine guns that are fixed so that they always point in the same direction as the main gun
CUPOLA
Round hatch in a tank turret, equipped with vision devices, enabling the tank commander to observe
DRIVE SPROCKET
Toothed wheel that is driven by the engine and that engages with the track, thus moving the vehicle
ESCAPE HATCH
Special hatch, not for normal daily use, close to a crew-man's position, and fitted with quick release to allow him to leave the tank by the shortest route in case of fire; sometimes found in the tank floor
FIRING PORT
Opening in the side of a tank or IFV through which the occupants can fire rifles or submachine guns; usually with a flap which can be closed when not in use
FUME EXTRACTOR
Tubular device half-way along a gun barrel that extracts the fumes after firing and ejects them from the muzzle so that, when the breech of the gun is opened to re-load, no fumes escape into the inside of the tank
GROUSERS
Metal plates clipped on to tank tracks so as to give extra grip in mud or snow
GUN
Main armament of a tank; usually taken to mean any armament greater than 30mm in caliber
IDLER
Freely-turning wheel at the opposite end of the track to the drive sprocket; it can be moved back and forth so as to take up any slackness in the track
IFV
Infantry Fighting Vehicle. Armored vehicle for the transport of infantry, similar to an APC, but with more powerful armament so that it can engage other IFVs and equipped to allow the infantry to fire their personal weapons while on the move.
LINKS
Individual sections of track; these are held together by pins which allow the track to be flexible. Spare links are often carried on the tank hull and turret where they give extra protection against attack.
LOUVRES
Slotted plates above the engine compartment of a tank which allow escape of engine heat
MANTLET
The moveable armored shield at the point where the gun passes through the front face of the turret
MBT
Main Battle Tank. the principal type of fighting tank
MUZZLE BRAKE
Attachment to the muzzle of a gun which deflects some of the gas emerging behind the shell, forcing it sideways and backwards, and so reducing the force of the recoil
MUZZLE VELOCITY
The speed at which a shell or bullet leaves the muzzle of the gun; measured in feet or meters per second
NIGHT VISION DEVICE
Sight or viewing equipment which allows the user to see in darkness; may operate by detecting infra-red rays or by electronic improvement of the existing light
PERISCOPE
Optical device which allows a tank crew member to see upwards and forwards through a layer of armor so that he can observe in safety
POD-MOUNTED
Refers to a gun carried in a small armored casing above the turret and remotely controlled from inside the vehicle
RETURN ROLLER
Small wheels which support the upper run of the track
ROADWHEELS
The main wheels which rest on the lower run of the track and support the weight of the vehicle
SKIRTING PLATES
Light armor plates which hang down outside the track to protect the track and suspension and which can cause shells to explode before touching the main armor

SMOKE MORTAR
Cluster of short barrels on a tank turret loaded with smoke grenades which can be instantly fired to give a smoke screen behind which the tank can retreat or maneuver if suddenly attacked in the open

SNORKEL
An air-tube attached to a tank which allows air to be drawn in and exhaust fumes passed out while the tank is beneath the surface of water; allows a tank to cross rivers and lakes with very little preparation

SPACED ARMOR
Technique of using armor in two layers, separated by a small gap. The first layer is penetrated but slows up the attacking projectile so that it cannot penetrate the second layer. Used during 1939-45 war but no longer, since modern methods of attack can defeat it

STABILIZER
Electro-mechanical device coupled to tank guns and sights that, when switched on, keeps the gun pointed at the target, irrespective of how the tank may swerve or bounce while moving across country

THERMAL SHIELD
Padded insulating material wrapped round a gun barrel to reduce the liability to expand and bend owing to the heat of the sun, which would render the gun inaccurate; also prevents a warm gun being detected by infra-red means

TRANSMISSION
Gear box and steering unit which accepts power from the engine and delivers it to the tracks

TRAVERSE
The amount a gun can swing from side to side to aim at targets; the amount a turret can rotate

TURRET
Rotating structure on top of the tank that contains the gun

Index